LATE FEES

A PINX VIDEO MYSTERY

MARSHALL THORNTON

KENMORE BOOKS

Published by Kenmore Books

Edited by Joan Martinelli

Cover design by Marshall Thornton

Images by 123rf stock

ISBN: 978-1729164068

First Edition

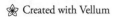 Created with Vellum

ACKNOWLEDGMENTS

I would like to thank Joan Martinelli, Randy and Valerie Trumbull, Kevin E. Davis, Nathan Bay, and Mark Jewkes and Louis Dumser.

1

I WAS LATE. NOT AN UNCOMMON OCCURRENCE IN LOS Angeles, but not one I enjoyed. I was on the way to LAX to pick up my mother, who would be spending Thanksgiving with me. Her flight had landed twenty minutes earlier and I was still a good half an hour from the airport. And no, the problem was not traffic.

She'd come in on a red-eye from Chicago, after flying out of Grand Rapids sometime the night before. Unfortunately, I'd forgotten to set my alarm. Always a restless sleeper, I'd rolled over and looked at the clock which read three—it took me a few seconds to realize I should have been on the road at two-thirty. That led to a frantic ten minutes before I bolted out my front door.

I parked in the structure for Terminal Four and ran across the nearly empty street. I hoped my mother had enough sense to stay at the gate and wasn't wandering around the airport looking for me. I entered the terminal, which was, not surprisingly, sparsely populated. A few people were lying around trying to sleep on their luggage, but a Moonie in a saffron-colored robe kept them awake thumping on a tambourine. I immediately ran up to one of the monitors for American Airlines and scanned it for my mother's flight. It had landed—almost an hour before. Taking an escalator up one floor, I ran to gate 45.

I hadn't seen my mother in more than three years. My life had been, well, challenging, and I hadn't wanted her in Los Angeles, and I also hadn't wanted to go back to Grand Rapids. Honestly, I wasn't sure what she might look like. She might have gained weight or changed her hair. The woman I thought I was looking for was sixty-three, small—almost bird-like, her hair dyed some shade of blonde, who wore sensible, classic clothes that tended not to go out of style.

When I got to gate 45 it was empty. That wasn't good. It meant my mother was floating around the airport. I needed to find a courtesy phone and have her paged. There was one on the wall at the far end of the gate.

I was about to go down there when I heard women laughing. I glanced across the way and saw two women in puffy winter coats standing at a bank of pay phones. One was tall, almost seventy, darkly brunette with a phlegmy laugh. The other was my mother. She'd let her hair go completely white and cut it in a softly curling bob. It looked good and that made me grumpy. Jealousy always made me grumpy. I'd gotten my father's unruly, misbehaving hair.

When she saw me she let out a squeal. "There you are! We were just calling you." She ran over and hugged me tight, enveloping me for a moment in a cloud of L'Air du Temps, powder and stale bourbon—the bourbon was new.

She stood back and looked me over, her eyes dewy.

"Oh Noah, look at your hair. Couldn't you do anything with it?" She looked flushed and her nose was red. Was she drunk? I didn't think I'd ever seen my mother drunk.

As I self-consciously patted my hair down with one hand, I said, "My alarm didn't go off. I had to rush out of my apartment."

"That's fine, dear. We've been having a wonderful time. Haven't we—Oh! I'm forgetting myself. This is Joanne. Joanne, this is my Noah!"

"Hi," I said, doubtfully.

"Noah! I've heard so much about you!" the woman said as she grabbed me and squeezed me harder than my mother had.

The purse hanging from her arm banged against me and clinked as though it was full of glass.

When she released me, she said, "You're right, he's cute as a button." I tried not to cringe but failed. I don't think there's a gay man anywhere who appreciates being called cute as a button.

"Joanne's son is late too."

"Did you meet on the flight?"

"No," my mother said with a giggle. "We met at a bar!"

That launched them on another wave of laughter. Then my mother took a deep breath and continued, "The layover at O'Hare was more than two hours, so after I found my gate I went into, what was it called? The Flight Deck?"

Joanne nodded enthusiastically.

"I went into The Flight Deck to have a glass of white wine —you know I'm a nervous flyer—and there was Joanne."

"She looked like a little mouse when she walked in. A little white mouse."

"Well, it's been thirty years since I walked into a bar alone."

I didn't know she'd *ever* walked into a bar alone.

"I just had to go sit with her," Joanne said. "There were some real mashers in there."

"Oh stop! No one was going to flirt with me."

"I don't know, Angie. I think if you sat in there long enough you'd snag yourself a pilot. Maybe two!"

That left my mother giggling and me wondering why we were talking about my mother picking up pilots.

"Anyway," she said. "We found out we had all these things in common."

"Like that we were both on our way to L.A. to visit our gay sons!" Joanne blurted.

"Isn't that a coincidence? When we got on the plane we found an empty row in the smoking section and talked the whole four and a half hours."

"Bourbon will do that to you!" Joanne said, shaking her purse until it clinked and clanged.

"Joanne collects those adorable little bottles."

"Empty or full, I just love them."

"Right," I said. "So, did you call your son?"

"Oh, I'm not going to bother. I know he's not home."

"You think he's on his way?"

"Are the bars closed?"

"Yes."

"Then he's on his way!"

"Um, but the bars stopped serving almost three hours ago," I said. "Last call was at one."

"Really? I thought L.A. was a civilized place? Why do they close the bars so early? That seems—"

"I think he should be here by now. You should try calling him."

Joanne looked at my mother who said, "It's only a quarter. And he might be there."

"Oh all right, sure, I'll call him."

She walked back over to the bank of pay phones and dumped a quarter into one. I glared at my mother and asked, "Bourbon?"

"With Coca Cola. At first. Really, Noah, don't give me that prudish look. You're not like that with your friends, are you?"

"They're my friends. You're my mother."

"Oh, pishposh. I'm a grown woman and I can do as I please."

I shrugged and said, "Okay. Sorry."

Then Joanne was back saying, "No answer. Why don't you two go on? I'm sure he'll be here in just a minute."

"Oh, no. We wouldn't think of it," my mother said. "We'll wait with you. Noah, can you find us some coffee?"

"Everything's still closed."

"Really?"

"Mom, it's not even four in the morning."

"Oh, something will be open soon." She looked around, then pointed to an empty gate. "Why don't we sit over there?"

"Shouldn't we go get your luggage?"

"Oh. Should we?"

"I should stay here in case Rod comes," Joanne said. I struggled to keep a straight face. She had a gay son named Rod. This whole thing was becoming more absurd by the moment. Maybe I hadn't actually woken up?

"Do you have a lot of bags?" I asked.

"Just one."

"Then why don't you give us your claim check and we'll get it for you," I suggested.

"Would you? It's a light blue Samsonite."

She dug through her purse for the claim check. This got my mother started going through her own purse. I waited.

"Oh, here we have it," Joanne said. She handed me two claim checks.

"You said you had one bag?"

"I do have one bag and a matching makeup case."

"Okay. We'll be back in a few minutes."

I gently pulled my mother away even though she was still digging around her very large purse.

"Noah, what *is* the rush?" she asked, then looked up. "Oh, this is a big city, isn't it?"

"It's not Grand Rapids."

"And someone could have walked off with our luggage."

"It's not likely, but it's possible," I said, as we started down the stairs to the ground floor. "And I wanted to get you alone for a minute. If Joanne's son was coming to get her I think he'd be here by now."

"You were late."

"I overslept. She said her son was out at a bar."

"But she doesn't know that. She's just guessing. He might have overslept too. I think you're going to like Rod."

The two things I knew about Rod were that he was gay and that he liked to stay in the bars until closing. I wasn't as confident as my mother that I'd like him.

We reached the ground floor and found ourselves right there at baggage claim. I checked out the TV monitor hanging from a thick pillar and saw that the baggage for my mother's flight was on carousel B. I picked out which one that was and led my mother over.

Carousel B was still going round and round, though it looked empty at first. And then a light blue Samsonite suitcase came out from the back. It was one of the big ones. Behind it was a caramel leather suitcase from the fifties. Even from a distance, I knew it was monogrammed in gold with the letters HDV for Harold David Valentine, my father.

"Mom, couldn't you get your own suitcase?" I asked, as we waited for the luggage to reach us.

"Oh, I don't think your father would have wanted me to spend the money. And I travel so seldom."

I pulled the two pieces of luggage off the conveyer and set them next to us on the floor.

"Do you just have the one piece?"

"No, I'm afraid not," she said.

Just then an even larger caramel suitcase, also from my father's set, came down the conveyer, followed by Joanne's blue makeup case. I grabbed them both and set them next to the other bags. It was a lot to carry.

"Can you take the makeup case?" I asked my mother as I struggled to pick up the other three bags.

"Oh Noah, you can't carry all of that, can you?" Then she whispered, "You're sick."

I'd told her in June I was HIV positive. Which was not the same as being sick, at least not yet, and it irked me that she'd said so.

"You're old," I replied.

"I'm not that old."

"I'm not that sick."

Of course, none of that made it any easier to carry three heavy suitcases at once. We limped toward the stairs.

"Why did you bring so much?" I asked. "You're only staying until Monday."

"I wasn't sure what the weather would be like."

"Speaking of which, aren't you hot in that coat?"

"Noah, it's freezing in here."

It wasn't, though. It was a climate-controlled seventy-something. Outside it was chilly. Well, California chilly: mid-fifties.

It didn't matter. I reminded myself my mother could dress herself however she wanted. Personally, I wanted to strip off my jean jacket. Carrying all that luggage was making me sweat. Halfway up the stairs I had to stop and set it all down. Any career aspirations I'd had to become a pack mule quickly flew out the window.

"I think we should offer to drive your friend to her son's apartment," I said, realizing that meant I could get stuck carrying the luggage right back down the stairs in a few minutes.

"You're sure he's not on his way?"

"We'll have her leave him a message on his machine that we're dropping her off. If he does get here and she's gone he might call and check his messages."

"But then he won't be at his apartment when we get there."

"True. We'll have to figure that out when we get there. We can't stay at LAX forever."

ROD LIVED in a slate gray building in Hollywood called The Pagoda. It sat at the bottom of a hill around the corner from the Hollywood Bowl. The eaves of the roof flared at the ends like a pagoda and there was an Asian-style screen in the lobby, but other than those two features the building was strictly mid-century modern: two floors of stucco boxes with metal crank windows. The top floor looked as though it had large balconies open to the hills around them. Below the two floors was a carport open to the street on two sides of the building.

By the time we got there, just before seven, the sun had fully risen. Joanne had insisted we wait at the airport another half an hour, and then fifteen minutes after that. We didn't leave until almost six.

During that time, I'd learned that Joanne had three children by different fathers: two of whom she'd married, none of whom she was with now. She'd raised her children, two boys and a girl, working as a grocery store cashier and picking up cocktail shifts in a bowling alley. As she put it, she was a salt of the earth, red-blooded American.

"I'm sure Rod has a good explanation and a funny story to go with it," she'd said several times by the time we pulled up.

"Oh you're right, Joanne," my mother agreed. "He's probably fast asleep in bed. Is he a heavy sleeper?"

"Not really." There was a tiny bit of concern in her voice for the first time.

I parked under a eucalyptus tree on the side street that ran up the hill next to The Pagoda.

"Have you been here before, Joanne?"

"Not to this apartment, no. Last year he had another place with his boyfriend, Scottie. They broke up after New Year's. Should we get my bag out of the car?"

"Why don't we make sure Rod's here first?" I suggested. I was tired of carrying suitcases and hopefully, when we found him, Rod would volunteer to come get his mother's bags.

Getting out of the car, I noticed that the open carport was nearly full. It being a holiday and early, most of the tenants looked to be home. That made me ask, "What kind of car does Rod have?"

"It's black," Joanne said.

Black was one of the most popular colors for cars in Southern California, that and silver. From where I stood I could see eight cars: five were black, three were silver.

"You don't know the make?"

She shook her head. "No. He was very proud of it though."

That was more helpful than it might seem. Rod probably drove a BMW or a Mercedes. Those were the cars Southern Californians were proud of; everything else was too Middle America. Jeffer and I had leased a little silver BMW convertible for a while, which I suppose we were proud of. He was, at least. But things change. Now I had a red Sentra, which I liked but was not proud of. I was, however, proud of the fact that it was paid for.

We walked up the steps to the lobby. As we did, my mother

asked Joanne, "What did you say Rod did for a living? Did you tell me that already?"

"He does something with movie scripts. I don't know what."

"You didn't tell me. I would have remembered that. It sounds exciting," my mom said, though 'something with movie scripts' was every bit as vague as driving a black car. Half the people in Los Angeles drove a black car and did 'something with movie scripts.'

"Does he work on set or at a studio?" I asked.

"Oh, no, he's right there with the actors. He's got stories about famous people." Joanne raised her eyebrows to make her point. "When we wake him up, I'll make him tell you a few."

"He's a script coordinator?" I guessed.

"Yes, I said that—didn't I?" She hadn't.

The lobby was behind a couple of large glass windows and a locked glass door. To our right was the metal panel of an intercom system that allowed the residents to know they had guests. Joanne scanned the list and found her son's name, BRUSCO. She pressed the button and we waited.

Nothing happened.

Through the glass I could see that the inner lobby had a row of mailboxes on one wall and was open to the courtyard. A large swimming pool surrounded by old-fashioned plastic strap-and-metal tube lounge chairs took up most of the space. I could see the doors to the apartments on the second floor; they were reached by an open stairway for each pair. For the floor below, the apartments appeared to have front doors down a few steps. Those apartments had some kind of terrace set a few feet down below the pool.

"He's not answering," Joanne said. She was finally beginning to seem concerned.

"What's his apartment number?"

"Seventeen."

I looked around the courtyard. It was easy to find apartment seventeen on the second floor, it was the last apartment to my left. It faced Cahuenga, a very busy street.

9

"We could buzz his neighbors," I said. "One of them might let us in."

"Oh we couldn't do that," my mother said. "It's too early in the morning. And a holiday."

"I guess we could go around the front and see if we can see anything. Maybe get his attention somehow."

We went back down the front stairs and around the corner, where we found four more parking spaces in the carport. In one there was a two- or three-year-old black BMW. It was covered in dust and dead bugs, desperately in need of a trip to the car wash.

"It's the top apartment, right?" my mother asked.

"Yes. The one on the end," I said.

We looked up. All we could see, though, were the railings. The top apartments had deep balconies, so you couldn't see the apartments themselves.

"Rod!" Joanne called out, trying not to be too loud. "Rod, wake up."

I went over to the BMW and peeked into the windows. The interior was tan leather. In the back seat, shoved into a corner was a stack of thin scripts looking like they were huddled there for safety. Yes, this was definitely Rod's car. The rest of the back seat was covered with old takeout bags, soda cups with plastic lids, loose mix tapes, an old pair of Reeboks, copies of *Frontiers*, empty water bottles and random gum wrappers.

"Rod!" Joanne called.

"Maybe if we threw some stones," my mother suggested. This from the woman who didn't want to wake the neighbors.

I realized I was being awfully nosey snooping around Rod's car, since I wasn't going to find anything that would tell me how to wake him up. Which didn't stop me from looking inside the car. In the front seat, a gym bag sat on the passenger seat. On the dashboard there was what looked like a drive-on sticker for Monumental Studios dated February 1992. I walked around to the other side and got a better look at the stack of scripts. The title of the top script was *They Come at Night*. It was hard to tell if that was soft-core porn or hardcore horror. Either way, I didn't think it was the kind of movie Rod's mother thought he was working on.

Behind me, the two of them had started throwing gravel at number 17. I needed to stop snooping. None of this was my business. Rod was going to hear his mother and wake up any second now. My mother and Joanne were certainly making enough noise. They pelted the balcony again, then Joanne yelled, "ROD! ROD, WAKE UP!"

I started to walk away from the car but noticed something on the floor of the back seat: a blue folder with the name KINGSTON INVESTMENTS embossed in gold. It caught my attention because nothing about the car screamed wealth other than the make. Was Rod really the kind of guy who had an investment portfolio? From everything I could see he was just another guy living well above his—

"WHAT THE FUCK DO YOU THINK YOU'RE DOING?!" a woman yelled from above.

I hurried out of the carport to join my mother and Joanne. I looked up and there on the balcony next to Rod's was a young woman in a red silk robe printed with blue flowers standing at the edge of the balcony with her arms crossed. The railing in front of her was lined with beer bottles and plastic cups. She'd obviously had a party.

"I'm sorry, I'm only trying to wake up my son, Rod, Rod Brusco," Joanne said. "Do you know Rod?"

"Your son is an asshole. Go the fuck away."

"Could you knock on his door and tell him I'm here?"

"No."

Okay, that was going to be hard to get around.

"Could you buzz us in so we can knock on his door?" I asked.

"No."

"Look, I'm sorry we woke you, but this is Rod's mom and she's just gotten here from Chicago."

"South Bend," Joanne whispered next to me.

That wasn't really relevant, so I just continued, "She'd really like to see—"

"He's not home."

"His car is here. How do you know he's not here?"

"All right, so maybe he's here. I really don't give a shit."

I was about to offer her twenty bucks if she'd let us in, when she said, "Look, he's not going to come to the door, he's sleeping it off. Now. can you just go away?"

"Was he at your party?" I asked.

She just rolled her eyes. "Fuck off."

2

_____

"I'm sorry to be such a bother," Joanne said, as we drove down Sunset toward Silver Lake. "You should have just left me there."

"No," I said. "I wouldn't do that."

It was broad daylight and it wasn't a bad neighborhood, but still, I wasn't going to leave a seventy-year-old woman to fend for herself outside an apartment building in Hollywood.

"It'll be fine, Joanne. When we get to Noah's you can call Rod and leave a message, tell him where you are and he'll call when he wakes up."

"I wish I could say this wasn't like him. He's never been the most reliable boy. But then he never had to be, he's always been one of those people—charm, I guess it is. He'll do something irresponsible and then the minute he shows up and smiles at you, well, it's hard to remember why you were mad."

"I'm sure he's a wonderful boy, and I'm sure he was just having fun and it got out of hand. Noah, why did you ask if he was at that party? She didn't seem to like Rod."

"I don't know, it just seemed logical. She said he was sleeping it off, so he got drunk somewhere and she knew it. Why she wouldn't want to admit he was at the party, that I don't know."

"I'll bet you're right. He was there," Joanne said. "Rod is so fun at parties. That girl probably didn't like that he got all the attention. Is that the Capitol Records building?"

It wasn't. Not even close.

"No. It's the Cinerama Dome," I said about the large, white, dome-shaped movie theater.

"Oh, I've never heard of that," Joanne said, sounding disappointed.

"It's an interesting building," my mother said. And a moment later she asked, "Is this where the riots were?"

"Some things happened up here, but most of it was a couple miles south."

"I was so worried about you."

"I was fine."

"Yes, but I didn't know that. How was Rod during the riots?" my mother asked, turning around in her seat.

"He saved a woman's life. She was just walking down Hollywood Boulevard and some black men attacked her. He scared them off."

"Was that on the news?" my mother asked.

"Oh no. Rod hates publicity."

I didn't say anything because the story sounded like a lie. Beating off 'some' black men in the middle of the L.A. riots seemed very unlikely. I knew that some buildings were looted on Hollywood Boulevard, but I hadn't heard of anyone being physically assaulted up that far.

"I don't know why everyone always says traffic is so bad in L.A. This is really not bad at all."

"Mom, it's a holiday. Everyone is at home or out of town."

"Oh, yes, I suppose that's true. I'm starting to get a headache."

"Hangover," I corrected.

"Noah, dear, there's no reason to be quite so accurate."

A few minutes and a couple of turns later, we arrived in front of my apartment. A small, boxy L-shaped building of two floors sitting on a hill about thirty feet above the street. A steep, red-painted concrete staircase led up one side of the property to the courtyard. I parked, got out of the car, and opened the metal mesh gate to my carport. Then got back in and drove my car into its space.

I was out before my mom and Joanne, opening the trunk. I lifted my mother's two bags out and set them on the ground.

"Joanne, do you need anything from your bags?"

"I'll just take the makeup case, I think."

As I took Joanne's smaller case out of the trunk, my mother grabbed both of hers.

"Mom, I'll take those."

"Noah, how do you think they got from the house to the car and from the car to the terminal in Grand Rapids?"

"Skycap?"

"No, I carried them. I can do it again."

I scowled at her. "Just one."

She picked up the bigger one and her bulky winter coat. It had warmed up and was now almost seventy, so she'd finally taken it off. I shut the trunk. Joanne didn't move to take any bags. We stepped out of the carport, and I shut the gate behind my car and locked it. Then I picked up my mom's smaller bag and Joanne's makeup case.

On the stairs, Joanne said, "You mother tells me you own a video store."

"Yes, I do."

"Do you think my Rod rents movies from you?"

"Um, he's a little out of the area. He might come by for something he couldn't find anywhere else, but other—"

"I'll have him take me by and show me."

"Well, we'll be open tomorrow."

"Does Rod have a lot planned for you?" My mother was right. She wasn't having any problems carrying her bag. I, however, was already winded.

"Oh yes. He has quite a lot planned. We're going to the Observatory, and the Hollywood sign, and Universal Studios for the tour, and the Chinese Theater for a movie—oh, and we have reservations at Spago for Thanksgiving dinner late this afternoon."

"That's a lot," I said. I'd barely planned anything for my mother. "How long are you staying?"

"Until Saturday morning."

Forty-eight hours? They were doing all of that in forty-eight hours? And he was starting off by oversleeping? Wow.

Joanne started to ask what we had planned for Mom's visit, but luckily we'd reached the top of the stairs, and as soon as we did I smelled bacon. I turned and saw my downstairs neighbors, Marc and Louis, sitting at the metal table outside their apartment right in front of a giant bird of paradise. There was a tablecloth over the table and it was set for four.

Louis was near forty, while Marc was about ten years younger. Louis looked a tiny bit like a frog and Marc was round everywhere. Both wore big welcoming smiles and their pajamas. Louis' PJs were a traditional red plaid while Marc's were baby blue with a floating pattern of black-and-white cows.

"Hello stranger," Louis called out. "We expected you more than an hour ago. Where have you been?"

"Louis, shush," Marc said. "You know how air travel can be. On a holiday no less."

"Guys, you shouldn't have done this."

"Don't worry, Louis was up doing prep for dinner anyway." We were having Thanksgiving dinner with them later. I wouldn't have been able to get reservations at Spago if my life depended on it.

"Well, this is my mom."

Marc and Louis stood up and came over. "Hello Mrs. Valentine."

"Angie, please."

"Angie," they both said.

"And this is Joanne," I said. "Mom and Joanne met at O'Hare while they were waiting for their flight."

"We figured out we were both coming to L.A. for Thanksgiving with our gay sons. What are the chances?" Joanne said, her voice loud and coarse. "My son was supposed to pick me up, but apparently he's fast asleep in his apartment. That boy.

He's the life of the party and sometimes I wonder it doesn't kill him."

"We stopped at his apartment on the way," I explained.

"He's dead to the world," Joanne said. "We couldn't wake him up even though we made a real ruckus."

"Well, sit down," Louis said. "We'll get another chair and some coffee."

"And plates. I'll get plates."

"We do need to make a phone call," Joanne said.

"Yes, we need to go upstairs and make a call," I said.

"All right. Fine. Put on your PJs if you want and come back down." Louis disappeared into their apartment while Marc went to find a chair.

We climbed the wooden stairs to my apartment, which was directly above theirs. My apartment was small, not even six hundred square feet. Walking in, the tiny living room was in front of us, boasting a fabric wrapped loveseat, a black leather chair from IKEA, an antique armoire holding my 13-inch TV/VCR combo, my video collection (or at least part of it), a compact stereo and a stack of CDs I'd gotten from a record club. Usually, a Hockney poster hung on one wall, but I'd taken it down and put up a photo from my parents' twenty-fifth wedding anniversary.

To our left was a Danish modern dinette set in front of the window. Beyond that, in what was meant to be the dining area, was an old metal desk under the corner windows.

"It's just darling," Joanne said. "Absolutely darling."

"Where am I going to sleep?" my mom asked.

"I thought I'd give you the bed and I'll sleep on the couch."

"Noah, that couch is too short even for you." She was right even though I'm not exactly tall. I was planning to put the cushions on the floor and sleep on them there.

"You raised a gentleman, Angie. Giving his mom the better bed. Such a sweet boy."

"We'll talk about it later," I said. "Joanne, the phone's right here. You can call Rod." I pointed out the cordless phone sitting on the black Parsons-style table I'd bought at IKEA. I think it was called LACK.

"Oh thank you," she said, making herself comfortable on the loveseat and picking up the phone.

I glanced at my mother. She was eyeing her anniversary picture. "Noah, can we get you something else for this spot? I mean, it's sweet of you, but you can't want to look at this all the time? I don't even have this picture up."

"Um, sure," I said, planning to completely forget she'd said anything since I didn't need a picture to hang there. "Why don't we take your bags into the bedroom?"

Joanne left her message for Rod while we walked past her into the bedroom. There wasn't much in there except for my queen-sized bed with a set of shelves behind it, creating a sort of headboard out of planks and concrete blocks. There was a window, a wall of closets and a built-in set of drawers next to the bathroom. There wasn't anywhere to put my mother's luggage but on the bed.

"It really is a sweet apartment, Noah. Very economical." She leaned in close and added, "You didn't need all that space anyway," referring to the three-bedroom house I'd shared with Jeffer.

"Thanks, Mom. Oh, I cleared out a drawer for you and there are some hangers in the closet so you can hang things up."

"Should I put my pajamas on?"

"You don't need to—"

"What's the number here?"' Joanne asked.

I gave it to her. She repeated it into the phone.

"Isn't that funny?" my mother said. "It used to be everyone had their phone number right on their phone. Now no one does. It's funny how much changes. Anyway, I don't mind wearing my pajamas, they're very modest."

"You know, we don't even have to go back down. You've been up all night—"

"Oh no, your friends seem so nice. And I am a little hungry."

"Oh, this room is adorable. I love the built-ins," Joanne

said, standing next to us and peeking in. "Noah, my pajamas are in my bag downstairs in your car."

"That's all right. I have an extra pair."

"We really don't need to—" I started.

"Go away, we need to change," my mother said, pushing me out of the room and closing the door. I stood there a moment wondering why my mother brought two pairs of pajamas for a four-night stay and then yelled through the door, "I'm going downstairs."

"All right, dear."

When I got down to the courtyard, Louis handed me a mug of coffee. "Well, well, you went to get one mother and came back with two."

I just rolled my eyes at that. "You didn't have to do this, Louis. How long have you been up?"

"A couple of hours. But don't worry, I wanted to check the turkey anyway."

The turkey sat just outside his front door in a giant pot soaking in brine. And, just to make things more complicated, the giant pot was in the center of a galvanized washtub filled with ice. They would have kept it inside, but there wasn't any room in their apartment, which had the exact floor plan as mine.

"So does your mother always pick up strange women?" he asked, unable to not tease me.

"No, she does not. They had a good time on the plane and then Joanne's son didn't show up, so we couldn't just leave her."

"Because there's no such thing as a taxi at the airport?"

Actually, it was the one place in Los Angeles where you could reliably find a cab.

"Louis, be nice," Marc said, coming out of the apartment with an extra place setting.

"It is strange that you couldn't wake the guy up."

"Maybe not. We met his neighbor. She had some kind of party last night. She wouldn't say, but I think he was there."

"Drugs or booze? What do you think?""

"One or the other."

"I drank a lot in my twenties," Louis admitted. "And I do mean a lot. I always woke up."

"Well, maybe it's both?" Marc suggested.

"They're welcome to dinner. When he wakes up."

"Thank you, Louis, but she's been promised Spago."

"Are you implying my dinner isn't going to be world class?" Louis said with mock-offense.

"No, but you've never been on *Tonight's Entertainment News*."

"Well, there is that."

And then my mother and Joanne were coming down the stairs. My mother had changed into lavender silk pajamas with cream-colored slippers while Joanne wore a very similar pink pair with her sensible walking shoes. Each of them carried a purse in the crook of an arm. Clearly, I was odd man out in my black jeans, red-and-white Rugby shirt and jean jacket.

Marc poured coffee for my mom and Joanne. "There's cream and sugar if you want."

"Thank you," Joanne said, diving into her purse and coming out with a tiny bottle of Jack Daniel's. She poured it into her coffee. "Angie?"

"Oh, I don't know."

"It will help you sleep."

"Well, maybe half."

As my mother poured Jack Daniel's into her coffee, Louis came out of his apartment with a large platter. Setting it down in the center of the table, he said, "Fresh biscuits with gravy, scrambled eggs, uncured bacon."

"Oh, it all looks lovely," Joanne said. "My doctor would kill me, but he's not here, so who cares." She grabbed the serving spoon and scooped out a pile of biscuits.

"I see we're being festive." Louis nodded at the Jack Daniel's bottles. "Marc—"

"On my way." And he scurried back into their apartment.

"So, Spago?" Louis said to Joanne.

She set down the serving spoon, her plate already stacked,

and said, "Yes. I'm so excited. Rod said it's impossible to get reservations."

"Almost impossible; you got in."

I handed the serving spoon to my mother and she took some eggs, a single biscuit with gravy and a strip of bacon.

"What does your son do?" Louis asked.

"Script coordinator. Monumental Studios," I explained, knowing Joanne would be vague. Then I put some eggs and a strip of bacon onto my plate.

"Monumental, huh?" Louis said, raising an eyebrow. Monumental Studios was one of the Gower Gulch studios that had a few sound stages, an office building or two and a handful of bungalows. Never one of the original big five, they now made the occasional low-budget, direct-to-video feature, but mainly rented out their soundstages to TV shows. And, yes, it was very unlikely that one of their script coordinators would be able to get a reservation at Spago on Thanksgiving.

"You can't only have that," my mother said, as she scooped a giant biscuit onto my plate.

I decided to be gracious and say thank you.

Marc popped out of the apartment saying, "Who wants a mimosa?" He had a bottle of champagne in one hand, with champagne glasses tucked between his fingers, and a pitcher of orange juice in his other hand.

"I'm fine," I said.

"Irish coffee is enough for me," said my mom.

"Well, I'll have one," said Joanne.

I took a bite of a biscuit slathered in gravy. It was really much better than I'd expected. I was eating more than I had been for the last few months, though I still didn't have what you'd call a healthy appetite.

"So, Louis," my mother said. "Noah says you're the cook today. What are your turkey tricks?"

"This year I'm soaking the turkey in brine."

"Oh, I've read about that."

"Last year he deep-fried it and nearly burned down the

building," Marc explained. "It's a relief that this year we're only facing possible flooding."

"I didn't nearly burn down the building. I scorched a banana tree. A little."

"Is there a grocery store open? Noah and I still have time to make something, you know."

"Oh my God," Marc said. "Don't even say that. We have so much food in our place it's ridiculous. Plus, Louis has everything timed to the second. Adding or subtracting another dish will just throw everything off."

Sensing he needed to change the subject, Louis asked, "Do you plan to do a lot of sightseeing while you're here, Angie?"

"Oh no, I just want to spend time with Noah. And, of course, I want to get over to see the video store."

"You haven't seen it before?"

"I've seen it once, but that was years ago. I know he's done a lot to it since then."

"Not that much, really," I said. Renovation was one of the excuses I'd used to keep her away once it was clear that Jeffer was sick and that he'd lied to me about, well, so much.

"What do you boys do for work?" Joanne asked.

Marc lit a cigarette, allowing Louis to answer first. "I'm in charge of accounts receivable for Eagle Rock Surgical Center."

"Is that a hospital?"

"Sort of. Not really. We don't have a trauma center and you need to schedule your procedure. We do a lot of plastic surgery and other electives. Fertility procedures that can't be accommodated in an office. Things like that."

"And what do you—" Joanne stopped cold and said, "Oh my God, you were on *Kapowie*!"

Marc's mouth fell open. "I was. How on earth did you know that?"

"I used to babysit my grandson, Bucky. My daughter's boy. He loved that show. You look just the same."

That was a strange comment since Marc looked like a guy in his mid-thirties even though he was still in his twenties. Did he look like a guy in his mid-thirties when he was on the show? As a teenager?

"Of course, Bucky's twenty-four now. He'll be out of prison in about nine months." No one asked why her grandson was in prison. It seemed impolite; and possibly something we didn't want to know.

Joanne turned to my mother and asked, "Are you sorry you won't be having grandchildren?"

"That's not necessarily true," Louis said. "There's a guy at work, he and his boyfriend are having twins with a surrogate."

"Really?" I said, a little surprised. I hadn't known guys were doing that.

"Oh yeah, they're very excited."

Of course, I had not even thought about children. I was really much more focused on surviving until my thirtieth birthday. Which reminded me, it was time for my AZT. I'd have to run upstairs after breakfast and take it.

The conversation turned back to Marc's career as a child actor. Joanne rattled off a list of famous actors asking if he'd met them. As though there were a clubhouse somewhere for everyone who appeared on TV where they got together and mingled. Talk then turned to politics. Joanne missed Reagan, which was awkward as the rest of us did not.

Upstairs, my phone began ringing.

"Oh thank God!" Joanne said. "That's Rod. I'm sure of it."

"I'll get it," I said, getting up.

"But he'll want to talk to me."

"Don't worry. I'll give him the address. He'll be here in half an hour." I left the table and hurried up the stairs.

I got into my apartment and picked up the phone on its eighth ring. I continued into the bathroom and opened the medicine cabinet.

"Hello?"

"Yes, I'm trying to reach Mrs. Brusco."

"Uh-huh. Is this Rod?" I took my prescriptions out of the medicine cabinet and shook the pills into my palm one by one.

23

"No, it's not Rod. This is Detective Amberson, Hollywood Division."

"Uh-huh?" A chill tickled the back of my neck. This might not be good.

"Who am I speaking to?"

"This is Noah Valentine."

"Are you related to Mrs. Brusco?"

"No, I'm just a family friend." And barely even that.

There was glass on the sink for brushing my teeth. I rinsed it out and filled it with some water while cradling the phone—

"Is Mrs. Brusco there?"

I swallowed my pills.

"Um, yes, she's downstairs. Did something happen?"

"I'm afraid I can only talk to Mrs. Brusco."

"All right. Hold on."

I walked out onto the balcony that ran along my apartment.

"Joanne, could you come up here?" I called down to the courtyard. I watched as she got up from the table and hurried up the stairs. This was bad. We'd left Rod's apartment building a little more than an hour ago. Best case scenario, he woke up, stumbled out into his courtyard and got arrested for drunk and disorderly. Worst case scenario—

"Rod wants to talk to me?"

I didn't have the heart to tell her it wasn't Rod. Wordlessly, I handed her the cordless phone.

"Rod, I hope you know I'm just livid—what? No, this isn't Mrs. Brusco. I don't use that name. Who is this?" She listened. "Yes, yes I am Rod's mother."

She listened again.

"No, no, he's sleeping. He had a little too much fun last night and he's sleeping it off."

Her mouth worked as she tried to say something more, then she took a ragged breath and let go of the phone. It bounced against her body and landed on the red tile of my balcony. She crumpled into a ball. I could hear my mother rushing up the stairs.

I snatched up the phone and said, "Hello? Are you still there?"

"Yes, I'm here," said the detective.

"Joanne just dropped the phone. She's very upset. Is he dead?"

"I can't tell you that. She'll have to tell you."

And that told me he was.

"I understand she was at her son's apartment earlier this morning?"

"Yes, she was. I was with her. And so was my mother."

"We're going to need to talk to her."

3

OF COURSE, WE LOOKED RIDICULOUS. FOUR OF US WERE IN pajamas. Right after I hung up with Detective Amberson, we piled into Marc's Infiniti and took the 101 up to Hollywood. I should have gone that way earlier but—forgetting it would be holiday-light—I'd assumed there would be traffic. I rode in the back with my mother and Joanne. Joanne wasn't crying, as I'd have expected, but she was pale, chewing her lip, and didn't seem to believe her son was dead.

"What exactly did the detective say?" I asked.

"He said that Rod had been found in his bed by a neighbor. But that's not possible. We spoke to that woman. She refused to even knock on his door."

It wasn't much of a stretch to think she'd changed her mind and decided to wake him up and give him a piece of her nasty mind. Obviously, we'd woken her. She would want to return the favor. I decided to explain that another time.

"Maybe it was a different neighbor," Marc suggested. Also a possibility.

"No. No. It's all a big mistake. I'm sure." Her voice had the sharp edge of panic. "A horrible mistake."

When we pulled up to The Pagoda there were three black-and-whites, an unmarked beige sedan, and a white van with a blue strip that said CORONER on the driver's door all parked in front. We had to park well up the side street and walk back down to the front door. My mom slipped her arm into Joanne's as we climbed the steps to the lobby. We stopped at the glass doors because they were closed with a uniformed LAPD officer standing on the other side blocking entry. I tapped on the glass.

"This is Mrs. Brusco. They called about her son." Too late, I remembered Joanne wasn't named Brusco, but I didn't want to explain all that. I hoped I wasn't being rude to Joanne.

The officer opened the door, made a small space, and waved her in, managing at the same time to shut the rest of us out. We could see everything in the courtyard, though, so we watched as Joanne walked through the lobby and lingered by the pool. At one of the umbrellaed tables, a handsome black man in his mid-forties, wearing a lightweight gray suit, leaned in to listen to the neighbor who'd so kindly told us to 'fuck off.' I guessed he was Detective Amberson.

When he saw Joanne, he nodded at the horrid neighbor and went over.

"That's the woman who lives next door, the one he was just talking to," I said to Marc and Louis. "In the red silk robe."

"The friendly one?" Louis asked.

"She was awful," my mother said.

We stood there staring at the back of her head while the detective led Joanne to another table. Just then, a guy of about twenty-five came out of number 16. He was model gorgeous, the kind of guy who really only looked natural next to a Hollywood pool or hopping into a sports car. He sat down with the woman, reached out and rested his hand on hers. She snatched it away.

"Someone having a pajama party?" a voice behind us asked.

We all turned to look at a shortish man of about thirty standing there with a grocery bag balanced on one hip. He wore drugstore flip-flops, a pair of Docker shorts with enormous pleats in the front, a lavender tank top with white piping and dark Ray-Bans. His body was thickly muscled in a way that made him look like a life-sized action figure. His deep tan suggested he'd never heard of skin cancer.

"We're here with Rod's mother," Louis explained. "Did you know Rod?"

"What's going on? Did something happen to him?"

"He's dead."

"Oh." The guy looked at each of us again and chewed the inside of his cheek before he said, "Pity."

Then he asked, "Are they not letting people in?"

We stepped out of his way. He knocked on the door. The officer cracked the door.

"Hello, I live in number 5. It's up that way," He pointed to the right, away from the pool. "Can I get to my apartment?"

"You need to talk to the detective first. Wait here please."

"Oh God." He set his bag on the ground. "Well, this is a disaster. I'm supposed to make a sweet potato casserole, you know, the good kind with the mini-marshmallows. That takes at least an hour and a half. Then I have to get ready. And I'm being picked up at noon! Noon!"

"It's eight-thirty," Louis said.

"I know!"

Ignoring all of that, I asked, "You didn't like Rod?"

"No," he said, drawing the word out like it was made of rubber. "Rod was fascinating, but so are rattlesnakes. No, I could not say I liked him."

"Did Rod have a lot of friends?" my mother asked, surprising me. It was a good question.

"None that he kept for long."

"Were you friends with him?" Marc asked.

"I just said I didn't like him."

"Not everyone likes their friends."

Number 5 swirled a finger at us. "Is this a new fetish? Three guys and an old lady in pajamas? I don't think it's going to be my thing."

"We were having breakfast when the police called," I said.

"So you just rushed right over?"

"He's dead. It seemed important." Louis said dryly.

"Tell us about your friendship with Rod," Marc said.

"We were only friends for about thirty seconds."

"What happened?"

"He's a user. He uses people for drinks. He uses people for drugs. He uses people to get to attractive guys. If you have something he wants it isn't yours for long."

"Used," I pointed out. "He used people."

"Yes, that."

"What did he use you for?" Louis wanted to know.

"Well, after he drank his way through half my bar, he thought he could help himself to my boyfriend. That was a deal-breaker."

"Are you friends with the woman next door to him?" I asked.

"Tabitha Hinsdale? She's even worse."

"So you weren't at her party last night?"

"Of course I was there. Everyone was."

"Including Rod?"

"Yes, Rod was there. He's always there, they're thick as thieves."

"This morning she acted like she hated him."

"She despises him." He glanced at our faces. "Don't give me those looks. One of you just said not everyone likes their friends."

"Who's the nice looking young man with Tabitha?" my mother asked. I thought it was another really good question.

"Allan. Tabitha's husband," he whispered, as if it were a secret.

That made Marc ask, "Oh really? Tell us about him."

"My, you are a nosey bunch. I might be offended if I didn't love to gossip." He took a deep breath and launched in. "Allan is an actor. And when I say actor I mean go-go boy. At The Hawk." He raised his eyebrows and winked at us.

My mother poked me, "What's The Hawk?"

"Gay bar. On Santa Monica Boulevard," Louis said.

To my mother, Number 5 explained, "They like to hire attractive straight guys. They think they're less trouble. They think they won't have sex with the customers, although that isn't always the case."

"Oh, my." My mother was getting an education. Not one I wanted her to have.

"So Allan's having sex with men?" Marc asked.

"One in particular. Name begins with an R. And you did not hear that from me."

Presumably, he was about to go in and tell all of this to the detective, who would be a lot more likely to mention it to Tabitha and exactly where he heard it than we were.

"Oh dear," I heard my mother say and then I looked into the courtyard. Two coroners were coming out of number 17. Between them was a gurney with a body on it under a white sheet. At the bottom of the stairs, they set the gurney on the ground and began to push it.

Detective Amberson stopped them, then said a few words to Joanne. She nodded and he lifted the sheet. I couldn't see much more than a lot of dark brown hair. A hand flew up to Joanne's mouth and she nodded her head. Her body was shaking. The detective dropped the sheet and rested a hand on her shoulder as she struggled to regain her composure.

Surprising me, my mother pushed open the door and brushed by the officer saying, "Please, she needs someone."

He stepped back, so I pushed through, too, just as the coroners were pushing the body through the door. My mother got to Joanne and slipped an arm around her. I stayed as close as I could.

"Who are you?" Detective Amberson asked.

"I'm Noah Valentine, we talked on the phone briefly. This is my mother."

He nodded. "You were here earlier with Mrs. Brusco."

"Lincoln. My last name is Lincoln." Joanne said, her voice hoarse.

"Mrs. Lincoln," he corrected.

"Ms."

"You were here with Ms. Lincoln. Why didn't you enter the apartment?"

"The lobby door was locked and that woman in number 17." I nodded to where she sat. "She wouldn't let us in."

"That's not what she says. She says she went down to let you in and you'd already left. Then she went to Number 17 and used a key she'd been given to go inside."

"She's lying. Unless I don't know the meaning of 'fuck off.'"

"She told you to fuck off?"

"Sure did."

"Can your friends verify that?" he asked, nodding toward the lobby where Marc and Louis remained.

"They weren't with us."

"I was there, and yes, that's what the young woman said," my mother said.

For a moment the detective looked like he might disagree with her but then he didn't.

THE NEXT FEW hours were chaotic, uncomfortable, confusing and very, very weird. We left Rod's apartment just before nine. Louis needed to take the turkey out of its salt water bath and get it into the oven. Joanne was dry-eyed and looked a little terrifying.

"Joanne, can you tell us what the detective said?" my mother asked when we were almost back to Maltman Avenue.

Looking out the window, she said, "It's not true. I know it's not."

"What's not true?" I asked as gently as I could.

"They think Rod took an overdose, but that doesn't make sense."

"Why don't you think it makes sense?"

"He wasn't—" She searched for the word. "—inexperienced when it came to drugs. I'm well aware of that. But he'd stopped. I'm sure of it. He told me he gave up everything except alcohol and marijuana. Months ago."

"And the two of you talked about that kind of thing?" I asked.

"Yes. We were close. When he was a boy I called him Pea because we were like two peas in—" She stopped and looked out the window again. I could see her realizing she was now a lonely pea.

When we got home there was the chaos of five people getting out of the car: Louis running up the stairs late to begin dinner, my mother asking if I could get Joanne's bag out of my car, my asking Marc if they had any kind of sedatives that we could give to Joanne only to have my mother answer, "I have Valium."

"Really?"

"My doctor gave me a prescription when your father died," she went on. "I brought it with me. Flying usually frightens me, but I met Joanne and we had such a good time I barely noticed we were in the air."

"Wait, are those still good? Dad died years—"

"I had them refilled. You know how I worry."

And then I realized the pills weren't about my father at all. They were about me telling her I was HIV positive. I had caused her anxiety. I hated that.

My mother led Joanne up the stairs while Marc and I followed. Joanne's bag was heavy. I regretted that I hadn't been able to get rid of it, though thinking that felt selfish. Especially since I knew what she was going through. Losing Jeffer wasn't the same as losing a child but it was complicated, confusing, hard to accept and ultimately devastating. He'd lied to me so much that I'd lost who I thought he was before I lost him. It became a double loss.

Was that about to happen to Joanne? She'd lost her son, was she about to find out she hadn't known him? She didn't think it was possible he'd overdose, but maybe it was. Maybe he lived more carelessly than she believed. And if it was worse than that, if he'd taken the overdose deliberately, how would that change what she thought of her boy?

At the courtyard, Marc said, "Dinner's around four. Drinks and nibbles at three. Joanne is welcome, of course, but if she'd rather not we'll send up a plate."

I nodded. The whole thing was terribly awkward. I had no idea what was right or wrong. Should we give Joanne privacy?

Should we stay with her? It was turning into one of those thorny Dear Miss Manners questions. Once we were in my apartment, my mother got Joanne a glass of water and gave her two Valium.

"There are things I should do," Joanne said.

"They will keep. Take these and you'll sleep for an hour or two. Then you can start with a clear head."

Joanne relented and went into the bedroom. My mother and I breathed a sigh of relief. Then we stood quietly in my tiny postage stamp of a living room until my mother said, "It really does seem endless."

"What does?"

"The city. Look at it," she said, nodding toward my view. "It looks like it goes on forever. Is it strange? Living in a place so large?"

I shrugged. "I spend most of my time in my neighborhood. Like most people I just stay focused on the parts of the city I use."

"That way it doesn't overwhelm you."

"I guess. On the other hand, whenever I want something I can pretty much find it." That sounded a little odd, so I added, "You know, museums and theater and music. Things like that."

She nodded agreement, then whispered, "Joanne hasn't started crying yet."

"Maybe when she wakes up."

"This is so awful for her. But I'm so glad we met. I keep thinking how horrible this would all be if we hadn't started talking in that bar at O'Hare. She doesn't know anyone in the city."

I almost said she didn't know us, but thought better of it. I'm sure my mother was also thinking what if it had been me. Who would be there for her? And that made me glad I'd had her come out, glad she had a chance to meet Marc and Louis so when—if something happened to me she wouldn't be with strangers.

"Well. What should we do?" I asked.

"Oh. Something normal. Can we watch the Macy's parade?"

"It's over."

"No, it starts at ten. It's almost ten now."

"Mom, it started at ten in *New York*. It was seven here. Time zone, remember?"

"Oh crud. That always screws me up."

"I don't think there's anything on television."

We looked around for the *TV Guide* but couldn't find it. When we gave up searching, I put *Miracle on 34th Street* into the VCR—I had my own copy. If we couldn't have the actual Macy's parade, we could watch a movie about it. I curled up in my POONG chair and my mother sat on the love seat. It was in the low seventies and with all the windows open there was a gentle, cool breeze. She snuggled under the red-and-black afghan she'd made and sent me for Christmas two years before.

During the opening credits, she whispered, "I am sorry. This is ruining your holiday."

"Mom, my holiday is just fine."

We settled in to watch the movie and were both fast asleep before Maureen O'Hara hired the real Kris Kringle as Macy's Santa Claus. I dreamed about my house, the one I'd owned with Jeffer. I dreamed I'd get to keep it if people believed that Jeffer was Santa Claus. That was awful since Jeffer was clearly lying about being Santa; for one thing his belly wasn't a bowlful of jelly.

He was skinny. Terribly skinny.

———

I WOKE up almost two hours later, the movie was just over and the tape automatically rewound with a thwap. Someone knocking at the door. I got up and opened it to find Marc juggling a cot that was already set up, a stack of sheets and a couple of pillows.

"Hi," I said.

"I hope you weren't sleeping. I just wanted to bring these up before I forgot."

"No, it's fine. Come on in."

He fumbled through the door. I tried to take a pillow from him, but it only threatened to bring him down in a heap. He set the cot on the floor, taking up most of the available space. Then he saw my mother sleeping on the love seat.

"Oh, I'm sorry, you *are* sleeping," he whispered.

"It's okay," I whispered back. "I'm awake."

He backed out of the apartment, quietly closing the door. I went into the kitchen and put on a kettle to make some tea. One of the few things I had bought for my mother's visit was a bag of mint Milanos. I got out a plate and laid out the cookies.

I was already exhausted and we still had a long day ahead. I tried to figure out if I was tired because I'd gotten up in the middle of the night or if it was my anemia. I had a pill for that, but I kept forgetting to take it. In fact, I decided I should take it while I was thinking about it. I turned to leave the kitchen, but my mother was standing there rubbing sleep from her eyes.

"Marc and Louis are very nice," she said.

"They are."

Then the water was hot, so I poured out two cups of tea and brought them over to the table. Grabbing spoons and the sugar bowl, I handed them to my mother. Neither of us took milk in our tea. I brought the plate of cookies out and set them in the center of the table.

"I can't believe I missed the whole movie," she said.

"Me too. We can try it again later."

She sugared her tea and then took a cookie.

"I should check on Joanne," she said, but didn't move.

"She's fine. If you listen at the door you can hear her snoring." Actually, you didn't even have to get that close. "Is Rod's father alive?"

"I think so. Joanne said she'd lost touch with him, so she's not a hundred percent sure. They weren't married. Of course, it was scandalous back then, having an illegitimate baby and keeping him. It's all so different now."

"She's lived a very colorful life," I said.

"The minister at Carolyn Harvey's church would say she's

getting her comeuppance. That she's getting what a sinner deserves. But that's ridiculous, cruel even."

"You're not still going to that church, are you?"

"Oh God, no."

We sat silently a moment, comfortably. "I keep thinking about when your father died."

My father had died about eighteen months before Jeffer. Heart attack. His third.

"I knew it was coming. At the time it didn't seem like that mattered, it hurt so much. But looking back I think it helped. I was at least a tiny bit prepared. I can't imagine what it must be like for Joanne, coming out here, expecting to spend time with her son and instead… he's gone."

In fits and starts, we chatted about some people she knew back in Michigan. I knew them too, but I'd been in Los Angeles for almost a decade, so anyone I knew in Michigan had faded and were now more like characters on a TV show I'd grown bored with than real people. They were real to my mother, though, and she talked about them with a lot of animation.

We'd eaten most of the cookies when there was another knock on the door. Without waiting for me to answer, Louis popped the door open and came in balancing a baking tray with two covered casserole dishes on it.

"I need to use your oven."

"All right."

He rushed in with the tray in front of him. At the stove, he turned the oven to three-fifty and slid the casseroles inside.

"I may have been a little ambitious this year."

"We really should have made something," my mother said. "You're doing so much work."

"Oh it's my pleasure. I always bite off more than I can chew. It's kind of my nature." He snatched the last Milano off the plate and said, "I'll be back in an hour for those."

He slipped out of the apartment and thumped down the stairs.

"We should get ready, I suppose," she said. "I'd like to take a shower."

"Sorry the bathroom's kind of in the bedroom."

"Oh don't be. It's a darling apartment and I'm glad you found it. Be thankful you don't have more space. I spend so much time cleaning and I wonder, why? There's just me to see it."

She went over to her suitcase, which had been sitting on the floor next to my lounge chair. Then I remembered again that I should take my anemia pill.

"I need to get something out of the bathroom first," I said, stepping over to the door.

Quietly, I opened the bedroom door and slipped into the darkened room. I went into the bathroom and opened the medicine cabinet. I felt my way around until I found my pills. On my way out of the bathroom, I managed to stub my toe on the door jamb.

"Oh, shit," I said, much too loudly, then whispered, "Sorry."

Joanne didn't budge. That seemed odd.

"Joanne?"

Nothing.

"Joanne?"

Still nothing.

I turned on the bathroom light so I could see better. She looked fine, just fast asleep. I opened the door to the living room.

"Mom, Joanne won't wake up!"

"Why are you trying to wake her?"

"I wasn't, I just, I made a noise…"

My mother came into the bedroom and looked at Joanne. Then she stepped over and nudged her. Joanne moved away annoyed but didn't wake up.

"That's not what Valium does to you," I said.

"Oh dear," my mother said. "Oh dear."

She hurried back out to the living room. I followed. She grabbed her large purse and pushed some things around until she found what she wanted. Her prescription bottle. "Oh dear."

"What did you do?"

"I mixed up my Valium with my sleeping pills. I gave her Halcion. Two of them."

"Sleeping pills?"

"I'm afraid they're kind of strong."

"You think she'll be okay?" I asked. It really wouldn't be good if we'd killed the woman.

"Oh, she'll be fine. My doctor gave me the lightest dose. That's why I take two. She'll wake up sometime this evening. I think."

4

MY MOTHER AND I STOPPED AT THE TOP OF THE STAIRS. The courtyard below us had been transformed. The metal table we sat around so often had been pushed up against a card table and the two were covered in a festive orange plaid table cloth, set with white dishes and silverware, butterscotch napkins and giant wine glasses. The table, the chairs, and even the ground were covered in brown, yellow, orange and red leaves cut from construction paper. Lights were strung from the bottom of the balcony to the bird of paradise. Marc had brought out their compact stereo outside and a CD was playing, Carly Simon's *My Romance*. It felt a little like being in a movie.

"Oh my goodness, I just thought of something," my mother said. "We should have brought wine."

"We've had a hectic day. I'm sure they'll understand."

The sky was cloudy and there was an occasional gust of wind. Standing in the center of the courtyard were Marc's friends Deborah and Rob. Marc worked with Deborah at the studio where they did something with numbers. Rob was her husband. I didn't know them well. She was short and little wide, whereas he was tall and pale.

Before we started down the stairs, my mother licked her fingers and smoothed down my hair over my right ear.

"There, that's better," she said. I felt about eight years old.

We went down the stairs. My mother wore a simple, brown sheath-like dress with low, conservative pumps. When she'd come out of the bathroom she'd whispered, "I have a nicer outfit, but it's pink and that just seemed wrong."

"I don't think we're expected to grieve for someone we've never met."

"Still, I want to be respectful."

"We don't have to whisper. Remember? You drugged her."

"You don't have to remind me."

I introduced my mother to Deborah and Rob. Then Rob pointed out a bottle of wine in a standing ice bucket—which made me wonder, *Where do Marc and Louis get these things?* Followed immediately by *And where do they keep them?*

"What kind of wine is it?" my mother asked.

"I don't know," Deborah said. "Something from Trader Joe's."

"It's a pinot grigio," I said, reading the label.

"Oh," she said, sounding disappointed.

"It's good," Deborah said.

"Is it? All right."

I poured out two glasses, and handed one to my mother. My anemia pill had had a little time to work, so I felt a bit perkier. Or maybe it was just the prospect of dinner.

"How's your brother, Deborah?" I asked, having met him the past spring.

"Oh, Jamie is great. Loving St. Louis."

"So he's not moving out here?"

"No. He's talking about moving to New York City, but I don't think he's going anywhere. He's really a hometown boy."

When he visited I got the distinct impression he didn't much like St. Louis. My guess was he'd be in New York by the end of the year. We talked about northern Michigan for a while after Deborah asked where my mother had come in from. Then my mother asked how they knew Marc and Louis, and was told that he and Deborah worked together at a studio.

"And what do you do there?"

"Ultimates. My department estimates how much a film will

make in every market and then we keep track of whether it does or not."

"Well, that sounds important. And you do that for every movie?"

"All six thousand six hundred and thirty seven. Most of them no one cares about anymore, but the numbers still have to go somewhere."

Marc came out of the kitchen. He wore a Hawaiian shirt he got at a thrift store over a white tee, khakis and a pair of mahogany Docs. In one hand he held a large plate topped by a folded cloth napkin, an orange and green floral that matched the table. On top of it were nearly a dozen tri-colored ravioli that had been fried in oil. A bowl of mayonnaise-based dip sat next to them.

"I've got nibbles," he said. "Fried ravioli with aioli. How is Joanne?"

"Still sleeping."

"That's probably the best thing for her."

"I think so, too," my mother said, avoiding my look.

"Who's Joanne?" Deborah wanted to know. An increasingly complicated question.

"A friend. Her son died last night. She just found out," my mother explained, impressing me with her brevity.

"Oh my God. What happened to him?"

"Probably an overdose," I said.

"These raviolis are great," Rob said.

"Aren't they?" Marc agreed. "I love when Louis makes them."

"Is Joanne a friend from Michigan? Or someone you went to school with?" Deborah wondered.

"I met her in a bar at O'Hare."

"Oh. I see."

"About eighteen hours ago, give or take," she admitted.

"Really? Noah, your mother is so much more interesting than mine."

"Wait until you meet Joanne."

My mother poked me in the side, the way she had when I

was a teenager. Just then, Tina arrived. She wore a baby doll dress in a black-and-white print, a pair of worn yellow cowboy boots and about twenty Bakelite bracelets on one wrist. Her blond hair was caught up in a giant clip at the back of her head.

Greetings were exchanged, Tina knew Deborah and Rob from previous dinners and she'd met my mother on a previous visit.

"It's nice to see you again, Angie," she said, giving my mother a Hollywood air-kiss, which she somehow managed to make sincere. Then she dropped her large, leather tote onto the ground.

"You don't have scripts in there?" Marc asked.

"Just two. I may need to sneak off and do a little reading." She lit a cigarette. "How was your flight, Angie?"

"Oh, the flight was lovely."

Marc got Tina a glass of wine while we caught her up on the Joanne situation. When we finished, Tina said, "How uncomfortable."

And, of course it was, particularly now that my mother had basically overdosed our guest on sleeping pills. Well, not overdosed exactly, but it was still unfortunate. Marc drifted off to get another plate of hors d'œuvres.

"So, she's been sleeping all day?" Tina asked.

I glanced at my mother. "Yes."

"I suppose that's a defense," Deborah said. "Against the grief."

"That's true," Rob agreed. "The mind works things out while we sleep."

Marc was back, saying, "These are miniature blue corn pancakes with caviar, sour cream and a bit of lemon zest. Just pop the whole thing in your mouth."

My mother took one, eyeing it curiously. Then, over my shoulder, Marc said, "There you are."

I turned and saw that our friend Leon had arrived. He was near forty, had dyed his hair platinum blond, and had a face that always looked a tiny bit pinched in judgment. He wore a lose rayon shirt with a black T-shirt underneath, jeans and heavy black work boots. I guessed that he planned to throw the rayon shirt into his car, strap on a leather wrist band, and spend the later part of the evening at The Gauntlet.

"Oh those look lovely," Leon said, making a beeline for the nibbles.

"We were just talking about the woman who's sleeping upstairs—" Deborah started.

"The one whose son died?" Leon said. "I know all about it."

"He called earlier," Marc explained.

"So, was he murdered?" Leon asked.

"Oh my God, no." I said.

"Why would you say such a thing?" my mother asked.

Just then Louis ran out of his apartment, oven mitts on both hands, and zipped up the stairs to mine. I was pretty sure I heard him say, "Almost forgot."

"What was that about?" Deborah asked.

"He put a couple of casseroles into my oven. An hour ago. Maybe more. Tell us more about what you do," I said, trying to avoid what I knew was coming next.

"Oh no you don't," Leon said. "Noah, why don't you think this woman's son was murdered?"

"Because it's much more common to overdose than it is to be murdered."

"His mother doesn't think that's what happened, though, does she?"

Wow, I thought, *Marc fit in a lot of detail.*

My mother took over. "She says he stopped taking drugs, except for marijuana and alcohol, and she believes him."

"A mother would, though, wouldn't she?" I pointed out.

"Well, yes," she admitted. "I imagine it's the kind of thing an addict would tell his mother."

"Lying well is a God-given talent," Leon said.

My mother put a hand over her mouth while she giggled at that.

"Just because his mother doesn't think he overdosed doesn't mean he was murdered," I said.

Louis came out of my apartment holding the baking tray

between oven mitts and balancing the casseroles. Carefully, he descended the stairs.

"Oh dear, that could go terribly wrong," said Tina. Since she spent her time reading movie scripts, I could see how she was trained to assume that a man carrying a tray of hot food while walking down a flight of stairs was inevitably going to tumble down into a comic heap at the bottom. But Louis made it to the bottom without incident and our dinner was undisturbed. We all breathed a sigh of relief and returned to our fitful conversation.

"I read in the paper today that they've had some luck treating AIDS with gene therapy," Leon said. "They think they may be able to give you a virus that will insert a defective gene into HIV cells."

"Give a virus to cure a virus?" Marc said skeptically. He switched from passing tiny pancakes to refilling wine glasses.

Leon shrugged. "It does sound a little far-fetched."

"They might as well inject you with the spaceship from *Fantastic Voyage*," I mock suggested. "Raquel Welch could cure AIDS with a miniature stun gun."

"If only it were that easy," my mother said quietly.

Leon wandered off toward the stereo. I sipped my wine; it was cool and crisp. "Do you like the wine?" I asked my mother.

"Oh, it's lovely. Very tart." I think that meant she didn't. She preferred sweeter wines.

"Are we going to see Louis at all?" I asked Marc.

"Is there anything we can do to help?" my mother asked.

"Yes, we should help," Tina said—the woman who'd brought something to read while someone else cleaned up.

"There's not enough room in the kitchen," Marc said. "Louis will be out once dinner is served. Don't worry."

"Really Marc?" Leon said, coming back from the stereo. "Five CDs and not one of them Barbra or Madonna? Sometimes I wonder if the two of you are homosexual at all."

"Who is this singing, by the way?" Deborah asked.

"Indigo Girls."

"Lesbian music," Leon said, dismissively. "All flannel and strumming guitars."

"Oh, I have to go," Marc said, as he'd just seen Louis waving him over to the apartment.

"I wish they'd let us help," my mother said. Determined to mother someone, she asked, "Do you think I should check on Joanne?"

"It's only been twenty minutes."

She frowned. "I'm sorry if I've ruined your Thanksgiving."

"Stop saying that."

"How did you ruin his Thanksgiving?" Leon asked. "Look at him, he's got a glass of wine in his hand and he's about to have a wonderful dinner—"

"I know but—if it weren't for me we wouldn't have Joanne on our hands and we wouldn't be talking about that poor dead boy."

"It's not your fault, Angie," Leon said. "Your son is the one who's a magnet for dead bodies."

"Mag— Noah, what does he mean?"

"Nothing," I said pointedly. I gave Leon a searing look.

"Well, he means something."

I sighed. "During the riots there was a body left in the dumpster behind my store."

"Oh dear. You never told me. Why didn't you—"

"And…" Leon said, annoying the heck out of me.

"And another time there was a dead body left here on this table."

"This table?" My mother pointed at the table we were about to sit down at.

"The round part, not the folding part," Leon said, getting unnecessarily specific.

"Why didn't anyone mention that?" Deborah asked.

"They did mention it, honey. They told us all about it, in September I think."

"What? Wait, no, that was a movie they were talking about. Wasn't it? You mean it actually happened? Like, right there?"

Marc came out of the house with a small tray holding four

soup bowls. "All right everyone, take a seat. We're going to start with soup. Carrot, apple, and ginger."

There were three chairs around the folding table and five around the round table. Everyone gravitated toward the folding table except Leon and me.

"Really guys?" I said. "It was months ago and all the dead body cooties have washed off."

My mother came down and sat next to me in the round portion. "You have a lot to explain," she said, under her breath.

As we sat down, Leon took a small, black mobile phone out of his pocket and set it on the table next to his setting.

"What is that?" I asked.

"Mobile phone. It's for work. Insanely expensive. Four hundred dollars last month."

"But work is paying for it."

"Well, they pay for the phone itself and all my business calls."

"How much of that four hundred was personal?"

"All of it."

My rent was only five-fifty. The phone at the store with three lines only cost a hundred and twenty-five.

"I'm going to be a lot more careful this month," Leon said, as though we'd all just scolded him. "Cross my heart."

Marc began placing soups; Louis was right behind him with another tray. As briefly as possible I told my mother the story of Wilma Wanderly and the blue-spangled dresses. When I was done, Marc and Louis were seated in front of their soup.

"See, that still sounds like a movie to me," Deborah said.

"It sounds dangerous," my mother said. "You have no plans to ever get involved with anything like that again, I hope."

"Not unless Joanne's son turns out to be murdered," Leon said.

"Even then. We shouldn't get involved."

"I agree," I said. "I've had enough of murder."

"Of course, there's nothing wrong with a little speculation," my mother said, making me uncomfortable. It always started with speculation—and then it didn't end well.

"Her son overdosed," I said firmly.

"In that case, the question is was it accidental or did he do it on purpose?" Leon asked.

"Did he have a reason to kill himself?" Rob asked, then added, "By the way, the soup is wonderful."

"Oh, it is. Delicious," my mother said.

"Nothing Joanne said would lead me to believe he had a reason to kill himself," I told them.

"But then is suicide a reasonable thing?" Tina asked. "I know we try to make it seem reasonable, but I think it's usually anything but. Did she say he was troubled?"

"She implied that he used to do drugs, heavier drugs than marijuana," I told the table.

"I don't think doing a little of this and a little of that means you're likely to kill yourself," Leon said, taking a spoonful of soup.

"If your mother knows about it, then it's probably not a little of this and a little of that," Louis pointed out.

"So he had a problem with drugs," I said. My soup was half gone. It was delicious, sweet and savory at the same time. "Louis, what is in this soup?"

"Oh yes, I'd like to know too," my mother said.

"Carrots, apples, onions, garlic and chicken stock."

"If he had a problem with drugs, then I guess he was troubled," Deborah assumed. "Which means he could have killed himself."

"But right before his mother arrived? That seems awfully cold," my mother pointed out. "If it was deliberate, I think he'd have done it after her visit, not before he even got to see her."

That left us quiet for a moment. It did seem awfully inconsiderate if he'd killed himself before his mother's visit, but then suicide was not a considerate act, or least not usually.

"And as far as we know there was no note," I said. "I think the police would have told Joanne if there was."

"Well, I'm voting for accidental," Leon said. "As long as we're sure it's not murder."

"It's not murder," I said, flatly.

We were done with the soup. Marc got up and began to clear the bowls. Louis started to rise and Marc said, "Sit down. I can do the salad on my own. You need a break before you carve the turkey."

Louis sat back and took a big gulp of wine, "Okay." Then to us he said, "I love it when he gets all dominant-like."

"Why aren't you with your family, Louis?" my mother asked, ignoring his risqué comment. I was thankful we'd moved on from suicide.

"My sister is in Texas," Louis said. "My mother takes turns. We'll have her at Christmas and then next year at Thanksgiving."

"And Marc, what about his family?"

"They're in Brentwood. Not on speaking terms."

"They don't like that he's gay?"

"No, they stole most of the money he made as an actor. Marc's touchy about things like that."

"As well he should be," my mother said. "I could never steal from Noah."

"You stole my U of M sweatshirt."

"You left it behind. And you never wore it."

"Well," Tina said, "my sister is livid that I'm here and not with her. But every time I go to her house she's livid about something anyway and then we fight the whole time. If she's going to be mad at me I'd just as soon not be there."

"Oh my you all have such complicated relationships. Not at all like Grand Rapids."

"That's not true, Mom," I pointed out. "The only difference is that in Grand Rapids everyone pretends to get along. They don't really know they have a choice."

My mother ignored the slight to our hometown.

"I saw something interesting in the news today," Rob said out of nowhere. "A panel the Republicans set up to investigate whether the Reagan campaign worked with the Iranians to steal the presidency from Carter—"

"Oh honey, let's not talk about that." Then Debra turned to us and explained, "He gets this way with a little wine."

"But it was in the newspaper just yesterday. The same people who committed the crime cleared themselves."

"But wasn't Mr. Carter terribly unpopular?" my mother asked.

"He was unpopular because he couldn't get the hostages out of Iran. During the campaign he was negotiating to get them released, but Reagan sent people over to make sure it didn't happen. That's why they wouldn't release them until after the inauguration. It's also why the whole Iran-Contra thing happened. Reagan had to pay them back by selling them arms."

"Oh Rob, please stop."

"She asked a question."

Honestly, I didn't pay much attention to politics. I had no reason to believe that Bill Clinton was going to be much different than George Bush. Leon came to the rescue by saying, "Do you know you can buy your own copy machine for a thousand dollars?"

"What do you want with a copy machine?" Louis asked.

"I don't know. I could xerox my junk and hand it out at the bars as a calling card. That's what the mail boys do at work."

"Other people talk about things they read in the newspaper," Rob said, before going into a major pout.

"Not everyone enjoys conspiracy theories," Deborah whispered to her husband. "They're an acquired taste."

Marc came out with a tray and began handing us our salads.

"Now what is this?" Tina asked.

"Field greens with blue cheese, bacon and cherry tomatoes, with a raspberry vinaigrette dressing," Louis said.

"Oh, it looks wonderful.

Marc set the plates down and zipped back into the kitchen for more. Then my mother said, "If Joanne comes down, don't anyone say anything about suicide. And definitely don't say anything about murder."

5

THE MAIN COURSE WAS FABULOUS: TURKEY, GRAVY, SAUSAGE dressing, mashed potatoes, sweet potato casserole, green bean casserole, creamed peas, mushrooms with onions, cranberry sauce and biscuits. Of course, Louis had to find fault with his own cooking.

"The biscuits didn't rise as much as I would have liked. That's why they look like hockey pucks," he said.

"But they're delicious hockey pucks," Deborah said, already putting a second buttered biscuit into her mouth.

"The biscuits we had for breakfast rose," I pointed out.

"I know. Go figure."

There were several minutes of near silence, all of us intent on filling our faces. I was nearly full after soup and salad, but everything looked so good I decided I had to have at least one bite of each dish. And then maybe another. My stomach was nearly bursting.

I took a break when Louis asked, "So Noah, since your mom is here, why don't you tell us about when you came out."

That was not expected. I had been afraid we might have to do one of those awful 'what are you thankful for' games where people went around the table and scrambled to think of something socially acceptable to say. This was worse. Not that it wasn't a common enough question to ask a gay person when you were getting to know them. Actually, I was sure we'd already covered this—hadn't we?

"Um, I guess I came out in stages. I was out to a few friends in college. And then when I moved to California I was pretty much out everywhere."

"He sent us a letter," my mother supplied. "I hope this doesn't sound too terrible, but it was very upsetting when it came. I just thought…well, I worried. It seemed like terrible things would happen to my son, which was awful to think about. I mean, the things people said about…" She stopped and took a sip of wine. "Noah's father decided we needed some time, so he called Noah and said that everything was going to be fine and we were going to take a few weeks to get used to the idea."

"And two weeks later she called me and everything was fine," I said, relieved to have gotten through it. Now it was someone else's—

"Why a letter?" Tina asked.

I shrugged. "I guess I couldn't face it if it went badly. I'd met Jeffer by then and it seemed like a good time to tell my parents. I mean, if they decided to cut me out of their lives I had Jeffer so I'd still have a family."

"You never told me that," my mother said. I'd clearly upset her. "What did we ever do that made you think we might cut you out of our lives?"

That stopped me. I sat there a moment with my mouth open. I thought it through quickly and said, "Um, nothing."

"Then why would you think that?"

It took me a moment. *Why had I thought that?*

"I guess it's that I grew up knowing good Christians threw their gay kids out and never saw them again. You and Dad were good Christians."

She looked at me a moment and then said, "Not that good, dear."

That got a few laughs. She reached out and took my hand. Then she turned to Louis and said, "This is such a lovely meal. And you made it all in such a small kitchen. I'm just so impressed."

"Thank you."

There were several more compliments and then Marc announced, "When I came out it devastated my parents. They thought I was going to make the transition into adult acting. They wanted me to be the next Tom Cruise."

Leon said, "No offense, darling, but you don't—"

"Believe me, I know. They brought me to several plastic surgeons when I was seventeen. They had a half a dozen procedures scheduled. I had to come out so they wouldn't chop me to pieces."

"That's horrible," Tina said.

"What's really horrible is that my coming out didn't stop them. They just assumed I'd stay in the closet and have all that crazy surgery. I finally had to threaten to call the *National Inquisitor* and come out to them. Not that I was ever famous enough, but '*Kapowie* Kid Queer' does make a great headline."

Leon's phone made a warbling sound.

"Is that your phone?" I asked.

"It is."

"Is it work calling? On a holiday?"

Leon frowned. "No."

He didn't pick up. When it stopped ringing, he flipped it open and looked at the tiny screen. Apparently, it told him who had called, like a beeper. He asked Marc, "Can I use your phone after dinner?"

"Of course. Can you wait that long or is it an emergency?"

"Oh, all right, I have a date afterwards. Is that a crime?"

"You could have invited him," Louis said.

"Just because I want to spend time with a young man doesn't mean I want to spend time with him. If you know what I mean."

My mother giggled again. Tina rolled her eyes.

I'd eaten all I could, so I pushed my plate away. Everyone else seemed close to being finished. Well, unless they took seconds. I heard a noise and looked up to see that the door to my apartment had opened and Joanne had come out. She held tight to the railing, looking unsteady.

Most of us at the table noticed that she'd come out and conversation died. In fact, everyone but Rob stopped eating. Marc jumped up and grabbed a folding chair that had been leaning against the outside wall of his apartment. He put it at the table between my mother and Tina.

"Joanne, come sit here. I'll get you a plate."

"Oh please, I don't think I could eat anything," she said, reaching the bottom of the stairs. Marc went over and guided her to the chair he'd set up.

"You should eat," my mother said. "Keep up your strength."

"Maybe just a glass of wine."

"Not with the Valium I gave you." Of course, what my mother meant was not with the sleeping pills she'd given her. She was a better liar than I'd ever given her credit for. "Louis, are you serving coffee with dessert? I don't mean to rush—"

"No, it's fine. I can put it on now."

Louis went into the apartment and we introduced Leon, Deborah and Rob, and Tina to Joanne. Instead of the usual 'nice to meet yous' there were several 'I'm so sorrys' and an 'I can't imagine what you're going through.'

"Thank you. And thank you for letting me join you. I hope I'm not too depressing."

"We're glad to have you. Are you guys finished or do you want seconds?" Marc asked. We all gave back our plates, except for Rob who went ahead and had a whole second plateful.

Deborah rolled her eyes and whispered, "I hate you" to her husband. Probably because he was one of those skinny boys who could eat as much as he wanted and never gain weight.

"Are the police sure it was an overdose your son died of, Joanne?" Leon asked. He didn't say suicide or murder, but it still felt like he was ignoring what my mother had said. I gave him a sharp look.

"The detective acted like he was sure. But I told him he was wrong."

"There's going to be an autopsy, though? "

"Leon, we should talk about something else," I said.

"Did the detective ask whether your son was depressed?" That was definitely not talking about something else.

"He did," Joanne said. "I knew what he was saying, though. He was saying Rod killed himself. But that's ridiculous. Rod would never kill himself. He loved life. I never knew a happier man. Never."

"What do you think happened to him?"

She looked at everyone at the table. "Isn't it obvious? He was murdered."

Just then, Louis came back to the table holding a gorgeous pie up in the air. "Coffee will be ready in just a minute. Until then, we have three-layered pumpkin pie." Marc was right behind him with plates.

No one at the table said anything.

"What's going on? What's happened?"

"Joanne thinks her son was murdered," Leon said. There was a touch of delight in his voice.

Louis set the pie down. Marc put the plates next to it.

"You're sure?" Louis asked. "It's easier to overdose than we think."

Joanne took her wallet out of her purse, then pulled out a couple of small photos. "This is my Rod. The one is high school, the other is more recent. When he went to Acapulco."

I took the photos and glanced at them. The high school picture showed an attractive kid with a mop of hair, unruly teeth and a strong, dimpled chin. The recent photo showed a very attractive young man who'd had a lot of good dentistry, an excellent stylist and the same strong, dimpled chin. Neither told us whether he'd been murdered. I passed them on.

"He loved life. Recently, he'd gone on a health food kick. I offered to make him Thanksgiving dinner, but he didn't want me to. That's why we were going out. He knew he could get something healthy."

I didn't think Spago had *that* kind of reputation, but—

"So you think someone murdered your son and then made it look like an overdose," Leon said.

"Yes, that's exactly what I think."

"So we need to figure out how exactly you do that."

"Force the pills down his throat," Rob suggested.

"But if you force pills down someone's throat there would be signs," Tina said. "The pills could have gotten stuck in his throat and then he'd die of suffocation." To Joanne she said, "I'm sorry, is this too gruesome?"

"I want to know what happened to my son."

"I'm just going to run and grab the coffee," Louis said, scurrying off.

"He might have fought back," Tina continued. "Scratching his killer and getting skin underneath their nails. The things they do now with DNA are remarkable. And they've completely changed the thriller market."

"You guys, we should stop," I said. "Why don't we go around the table and say what we're grateful for?"

"Someone might have slipped drugs into his food," Deborah offered. "You know, ground up some pills."

"That would depend on what kind of overdose you were faking," Marc said to Deborah. "Stomach contents are checked during an autopsy, so if they're expecting pills or capsules there wouldn't be any. I think people die before they have time to dissolve completely."

"Where did you learn that? *Quincy*?" Leon asked.

"Yes, actually. I did an episode in the second season. I mean, it wasn't about faking an overdose. I was an evil child who pushed his twin off a cliff. After my episode I got hooked on the show and watched it all the time."

"Someone could have just held him down and injected him," Leon said.

"They'd need an accomplice," Marc said.

"Could there have been an accomplice?"

We all looked at one another; we had no idea. Louis came back with a tray and coffee. Marc began passing out cups.

"What did I miss?" Louis asked.

"DNA. Stomach contents. *Quincy*. And an accomplice."

"Are you okay?" I asked Joanne. "This can't be pleasant."

"An accomplice just means you're more likely to get caught," she said. "Just ask my Bucky. Eventually they turn on you."

Louis began pouring coffees. Deborah put her hand over her cup, "Oh no, I'll never get to sleep."

"This conversation is probably going to keep me awake," Tina said.

"Joanne, how big was your son?" Leon wanted to know. "I think I could hold a small person down and inject them with a lethal dose of horse."

"Horse? Are you visiting from the seventies?" Marc asked.

"Shush," Leon replied.

"Rod was tall. Almost six foot."

"And, he'd just come from a party," Leon said. "Maybe he was drunk enough that someone could hold him down and inject him."

"Noah, two questions," Louis said. "Do *you* think Rod was murdered? And would you like pie?"

"I would like pie." His first question hung in the air. I didn't want to encourage Joanne. It didn't seem healthy. "I'm not sure I can answer your first question until we know what the autopsy says."

"Can we try to find that out?" Joanne asked.

Louis put the coffee pot down and cut me a slice of pie. He handed it to Rob who passed it down the table.

"We could call the detective you spoke to," my mother suggested. "Maybe he could tell us."

"He's not likely to tell you anything," Leon said. "In general the LAPD is not very friendly. Just ask Rodney King."

"Angie, would you like pie?" Louis asked.

"Yes, thank you."

"Noah?" Leon asked.

"What? I have pie." I would have taken a bite too, but the conversation was tying my stomach into a Gordian knot.

Leon raised his eyebrows in a question.

I knew what he wanted me to do, so I said, "No."

"No to what?" my mother asked.

"We know a policeman," Marc said, sitting down and pulling out his cigarettes.

"Could I have one of those?" Joanne asked. "I gave it up years ago, but right now I can't remember why."

Marc offered his pack and lighter.

"Noah, you know a policeman?" my mother asked, obviously surprised. And why shouldn't she be? There was a lot I hadn't told her. She studied me. "How do you know—oh wait, is he—"

"Yes, he is. Very," Leon said. "Isn't he, Noah?"

"It's not his case. It's not even his precinct. Or district. Whatever they call it. So there's no reason to contact him. He wouldn't—"

"He might be willing to help," Leon said.

"It never hurts to ask," my mother threw in.

I wondered if I could strangle them both and claim justifiable homicide.

"HE WAS SUCH A WONDERFUL BOY. Mm-hmmm. Mm-hmmm. I know. Yes. I have no idea what I'll do without him. I really don't," Joanne said into the cordless phone. She was sitting at my dining table, which was only a few feet from where I'd been sleeping on the uncomfortable canvas cot Marc had brought up. I rolled over and sat up.

"I don't know. I haven't made any plans. I might do something here for his friends and something at home for family. It just depends."

After all the wine I'd had the night before I had a very nasty headache. I stumbled into the kitchen for a glass of water. The orange digital clock on my stove said 7:20. God, I wanted to go back to sleep. Desperately.

My mother came and stood at the edge of the kitchen. There really wasn't room for the two of us to be in there at the same time.

"Do you want a glass of water?" I asked her.

"Please." She held out her open palm and showed me four white pills.

"And those are?" I asked, raising an eyebrow.

"Aspirin. Don't worry, I looked at the bottle."

I poured her a glass of water and then took two of the aspirin from her palm. We swallowed our aspirin and drank down our glasses of water. Like mother, like son.

"No, I've got everything handled for the moment. I really just have to wait until the police release—"

"What should we do today?" I asked my mother quietly as I refilled our waters.

She whispered back, "I think we should find out what Joanne needs before we decide."

"She needs a funeral home, don't you think?"

"I suppose." I could tell she was thinking about how to bring this up. The police were holding the body, but at some point they'd release it and it would need to go somewhere.

"I need coffee," I said, pulling my Mr. Coffee away from the wall and opening the lid. Then I looked in the cupboard to see if I had any Maxwell House. There was a knock on the door.

My mother said, "I'll go."

I listened to see who it was, assuming it would probably be Marc or Louis, but all I heard was Joanne on the phone. "Do you have the number for the warden at Putnamville? I have to reach Bucky."

Then my mother was back holding a tray with three cups of coffee and three slices of pumpkin pie. We'd finished the first pie the night before and then Louis produced a second identical one, which we were too full to even consider. It seemed decadent to have pie for breakfast. But then, there was a woman in my living room trying to reach her grandson in prison. That was hardly wholesome.

My mother slipped the pie and coffee in front of Joanne, then we huddled in the kitchen with ours. The pie was three layers: a regular pumpkin pie filling at the bottom, a creamier pumpkin filling in the center, and whipped cream on top with

sprinkled pecans. Each forkful was smooth and spicy, and sometimes crunchy.

I was nearly finished with my piece, when I said to my
mother, "When I talk to Javier I'll ask if he can find out when
they'll release the body."

"And Javier is?"

"Oh. Sorry. Detective Javier O'Shea."

"Are you dating him?"

"No. No. I haven't seen him since the whole Wilma
Wanderly fiasco."

"So, is that when you met him?"

"No, I met him right after the riots. I told you, this guy I
knew died. I mean, actually he didn't die, well, no he did, just
not when we thought."

"He's the man who was found in your dumpster?"

"Yes."

My mother studied at me. "We're going to have to have a
long talk about all of this."

"The pie is really good, isn't it?" I asked, clever change of
subject on my part.

"All right darling. Thank you. I love you too," Joanne was
saying.

It sounded like she was hanging up. I stepped by my mother
and said, "Joanne, I need to make a call."

"Oh, of course. I'm getting a little tired anyway." She held
out the cordless phone to me.

"It's all so hard."

"It is. So hard."

"Are your other children flying out to help?" my mother
asked.

"Oh they want to, but I told them no. Cindy just had the
twins and Billy can't leave his job at the Pizza Hut."

I picked up the phone and went into the bedroom, as my
mother asked, "Doesn't Cindy have a twenty-four year-old?"

"She does, Billy. She was fifteen when she had him and
thirty-seven when she had the twins. She'd be a grandmother by
now if Billy hadn't spent so much time behind bars."

"Well, twins are a handful," my mother said.

"Don't I know it. I practically raised Billy for her. and when she started those fertility treatments I made it clear I wasn't raising any more of her children. She did not like hearing that."

I found the pants I'd had on the day before and got out my wallet. In it was Javier's card tucked behind my May Company charge card. I suppose it was silly to keep his card in my wallet, but there it was, like a get-out-jail-free card. On the back of it was his beeper number. I dialed and input my phone number. I wondered if he'd know it was me calling.

"Joanne, should we be thinking about arrangements?" my mother asked carefully.

"The detective said he wasn't sure when—when we could have Rod."

"Still there might be a few things we could do just to feel like we've accomplished something. We could pick out a funeral parlor and then they'll take care of everything for you. Do you know if Rod wanted to be cremated or buried?"

"I don't know. I don't remember him saying. We didn't talk about those things."

I walked back into the living room in time to ask, "Do you think he'd want to be here or in South Bend?"

"I don't know. I really don't. I hate to think of him far away, but then he loved it here. I hate to take him away from a place he loved."

"If it turns out—"

The phone rang in my hand. Quickly, I stepped out onto the balcony running along my apartment.

"Noah? You beeped me?" I couldn't help feeling just a little happy that he knew my phone number by heart.

"I did."

"It's nice to hear from you."

That made me smile. I wanted to say it was nice to talk to him too—but I couldn't. That would be wrong.

"I'm calling for a favor," I said quickly, knowing he'd be angry if I let him get the wrong idea.

"Oh. Yes, of course you are."

63

His tone stung and I wanted to say 'don't be like that' but why shouldn't he be like that? I knew he liked me; he'd kissed me in broad daylight on Santa Monica Boulevard. And then, well, nothing. I'd made sure of that. He had every right to be testy. He had every right not to call me back.

"My mother's here visiting and she met this woman—"

"Your mother's a lesbian?"

"No. That's not where this is going."

"Okay."

"My mother became *friends* with a woman on the flight out. And that woman's son died yesterday morning. They think it was an overdose, but she's adamant—"

"And you want me to take a peek at the autopsy?"

"If you could."

"Where did this happen?"

"Hollywood."

"And the guy's name?"

"Rod Brusco."

"I'm going to have to call in a favor. Is this worth it?"

I paused for a moment. Was he asking if I was going to make it worth his while? Was I being bribed? I mean, not for money, obviously but—

I couldn't tell. Finally, I said, "His mother is sweet. She's seventy-something and kind of a character. She thinks her son was murdered. It's probably an accidental overdose, so the sooner she understands that the better it will be for her. Don't you think?"

He was silent long enough that I was sure he was about to tell me to forget it. Instead, he said, "Meet me at The Living Room. Four o'clock."

6

When I went back inside, Joanne asked, "Can you take me to Rod's? I should stay there. Get out of your hair."

"Do you think you can?" I asked. "I mean, it might still be taped off."

"They told me they'd be finished by this morning."

"You are welcome to stay here longer if you need to."

"Oh that's so kind, but I'd like to be at Rod's. I'll feel closer to him."

"We could go with Joanne," my mother said. "And then pop by the video store afterward."

"We could…" I said, though I was considering a little sight-seeing over that way, since we were going.

About forty-five minutes later we were cleaned up and ready to go back to Rod's apartment. As we left my apartment, U2 was wailing 'please come home' from downstairs. Marc and Louis' stereo was still outside and they were playing *A Very Special Christmas*—I had the same CD. The courtyard was in the process of being transformed. They were putting up blinking Christmas lights, stringing them from the underside of my balcony to the tip-top of the bird of paradise. From the string of lights, they were hanging glittery ornaments.

"Merry Christmas!" Louis said when he saw us.

"Guys!" I said. "It's still November."

"It's the holiday season," Marc said. "Be of good cheer. 'Tis the season, blah-blah-blah."

Ignoring his lover, Louis asked, "Where are you off to?"

Chatting with them was a good excuse to put Joanne's bag down and take a slight break before the next flight of stairs. "Joanne is leaving to stay in Rod's apartment."

"Oh, I see," Louis said. He seemed as concerned as I was. "Well, I hope we see you again."

"Thank you so much for your kindness," Joanne said.

"Don't be silly. We didn't do a thing."

That was not strictly true.

I picked up Joanne's suitcase again and said, "We should get going."

The three of us started down the stairs, but then my mother said, "One second," and ran over to Marc and Louis. From where I was on the stairs I couldn't exactly hear what she said to them. But I did hear Louis say, "That sounds great."

Whatever *that* was.

A moment later my mother was back with us and we continued down to the street.

"What was that?" I asked.

"We're taking them to dinner tonight. It only seems right after all the work they did yesterday." She was very happy with herself. "My treat."

"Did you talk to your policeman friend?" Joanne asked.

"Yes. He's going to find out what he can. We're meeting for coffee later this afternoon."

"You'll call me and let me know what he says?"

"Of course."

While I got the car out of the carport, Joanne and my mother exchanged phone numbers so I'd know where to call. The drive over to Rod's apartment was quiet. There wasn't a whole lot to say at that particular moment. Sightseeing seemed trivial, so I didn't point out the things I might have had my mother and I been alone. In fact, everything seemed trivial compared to losing a son.

I did begin to wonder if there was a reason I didn't want to view Rod's death as a murder. A reason that had nothing to do with the facts. I had really had a lot of murder in the last year. An accidental overdose would be a relief. But I shouldn't let my own prejudices and desires color my conclusions. Yes, it would be nice to go through the rest of my life and never talk about another murder case. But was that even possible? Just watching the news brought us all—

"I really enjoyed your friend Leon," my mother said. I wasn't sure Joanne could hear much in the backseat.

"He's really more Marc and Louis' friend," I said.

"So there's no possibility there?"

"Oh God no."

"I just thought—well, he was teasing you about that police-man. It seemed like jealousy, that's all."

"It's not. Believe me. He teases everyone."

"All right."

"So what exactly is going on with your policeman?"

"Nothing. Exactly nothing," I said forcefully enough to end conversation for the final two miles. I glanced in the rearview mirror. Joanne seemed lost in thought and not at all concerned about my love life, which was fine with me.

I parked on the side street again under the same eucalyptus tree. A man in his early forties with jet black hair and deeply tanned skin the color of bricks was hosing down the carport. I had a feeling that was against the law since we were still in a drought. He should have swept it instead. No one would say anything, though, I was pretty certain. No one ever did.

"Are you Eddie?" Joanne asked, surprising me.

"I am." He seemed almost as surprised as I was.

"I'm Rod's mother. He told me all about you."

"Mrs. Brusco, I'm so sorry."

"Joanne, please."

"Joanne."

"These are my friends, Angie Valentine and her son, Noah."

He nodded at us. "Eddie Castellon. I own the building." He wore a pair of baby blue shorts, a white golf shirt and a pair of drugstore flip-flops. He turned off the hose and set it down at the bottom of the stairs.

"I was hoping we'd find you. I don't have a key to Rod's apartment. I was here yesterday when they found him. Honestly, I was too flustered to ask the police to give me his keys."

"Of course," Eddie said, though to what I wasn't sure. "Why don't you follow me."

We followed him to what I realized was another entrance to the building between two sections of the carport. We climbed up a narrow staircase to a screened security door. Eddie took a ring of keys that were hooked to his belt and found the one that opened this door. That led us into the courtyard above the pool.

"Sorry to hear about Rod. I didn't know him that well, but he was always very friendly whenever I'd see him around the building."

"So you live here, Mr. Castellon?" my mother asked.

"I do. My wife and I have one of the two-bedrooms up this way."

Now I could see that The Pagoda was actually two buildings. The outer building followed Cahuenga and whatever the side street was called (I hadn't seen a sign), forming a kind of lazy U. And inside that, a simple two-story square building that contained at least six apartments.

"We didn't see you yesterday," I said.

"We were in San Diego for the holiday. Went down Wednesday night. My wife's family." He'd mentioned his wife twice. I wondered if he was uncomfortable with Rod's being gay. Or maybe it was me he was uncomfortable with. He led us up to the apartment at the front of the second floor. We climbed a flight of stairs and then walked along an open walkway similar to the one outside my apartment.

"Come in, come in," Eddie said.

Inside, the apartment had a cathedral ceiling, large living room, minuscule kitchen, and a hallway that led down to the mentioned two bedrooms. On one side of the living room was a desk with a pegboard hung on the wall next to it. The pegboard seemed to hold keys to every apartment in the building. There was a sectional sofa in the living room and a marble coffee table. Everything was covered with toys, and between the living room area and the dining room area was a playpen with two small children in it. One and two? Maybe two and three? I was a terrible judge of children's ages.

A woman came down the hall. She was small and pretty with dark, straight hair. A boy of around five held onto her as she walked. "Eddie, can you take him? He's being clingy again."

She wore a gray, pin-striped business suit. In the hand that wasn't holding her son, she carried a pair of conservative black pumps. When Eddie stepped forward and took the boy, she dropped the shoes onto the floor and stepped into them.

"I have to hurry, I'm already a half an hour late."

"Consuelo, this is Rod's mother."

"Oh. Oh my. It's so very sad about your son. We had no idea he was that involved in drugs. Perhaps if we'd known—"

"He wasn't involved in drugs. He'd stopped. I'm sure—"

"You're visiting from out of town, Joanne?" Eddie asked as he took a key off the wall and gave it to her.

"Yes, I'm from Indiana."

"I imagine this changes your plans."

"It does."

Consuelo kissed her husband on the cheek and said, "Going now. I'll call you after lunch."

"All right sweetheart."

Consuelo hurried out of the apartment. Still holding his son, Eddie said, "Shall we?"

"Oh you don't need to," I said reflexively. I glanced at the two kids in the playpen. "We can bring the key back to you."

"They'll be fine for five minutes. Trust me, there's only so much attention you can pay to three kids even when you're in the room."

I glanced at my mother who was frowning—I didn't think she agreed—as we followed Eddie, still carrying his oldest, out of the apartment. Joanne asked, "What does your wife do?"

"She's a public defender. You'd think she'd have the day off since the court is closed, but she's got a half dozen meetings."

"Well, I think she's doing very important work. The public defender my grandson had was very good. He very nearly got Bucky off. Not that he'd done anything *that* wrong. The gun wasn't even loaded."

We all just smiled. The boy whispered into this father's ear. "Yes, Manny, you can have a cookie when we get back. But only if you're really good."

The boy whispered in his father's ear again. Eddie chuckled. Then, as he led us up Rod's steps, he said, "I know this may be awkward, but Rod was a month behind on his rent. I can keep the security deposit so it's not a big deal, but I do need to rent the apartment as soon as I can."

"I understand," Joanne said. "I'm not planning to stay long. Are you sure he was behind, though? I mean, he had money. He paid for my plane ticket."

"From what I've heard that sounds like Rod. Being broke never seemed to stop him from spending money."

We climbed the stairs down to the courtyard.

"But Mr. Castellon, no, Rod wasn't broke. He made a good living and he inherited a lot of money from a dear friend just a few years ago."

"You know when he moved in ten months ago I ran his credit and it seemed fine or I wouldn't have let him in. But he has been late three times on his rent."

"Well, I'm sure it was just sloppiness. He was never a very organized boy."

Eddie smiled at that. I couldn't tell if the smile meant he understood or that he thought she was misunderstanding the situation. We climbed the steps up to number 17. He bounced his son a few times and made him giggle.

Then he opened the door for us and we stepped into the apartment. Inside, it was similar to the Castellon's unit. They both had the same cathedral ceilings. Rod's apartment had a smaller, narrow living room, and a tiny kitchen that was almost an afterthought. Sliding glass doors opened onto an enormous balcony, which was nearly as large as the entire apartment.

In the living room, there was a black leather sofa, a glass coffee table, a leather occasional chair, a large black Sony Trinitron sitting on a black stand, and a makeshift desk—two filing cabinets topped by a door—under the window that looked out into the courtyard. On the desk was a white, portable Macintosh computer—at that point I stopped. There was a lot of money in this room. Or at least there had been when everything was originally purchased. It wouldn't be worth nearly as much secondhand.

We were hearing conflicting things about Rod. In one story he seemed to be very comfortable financially, in another he was scrambling for money. Was everything purchased on credit? Or had he had money and spent it all? Or was he just really sloppy about things like that?

On the glass coffee table I noticed an open wooden box, carved, probably from Pier One, with rolling papers inside and nothing else. Next to the box, there was a clean circle on the dusty glass surface. A bong had once sat there. And in the box there had probably been a pipe and a plastic sandwich bag filled with marijuana. All of it had been taken by the police as evidence. Though I had to wonder if it really was evidence. And, if so, evidence of what?

"Oh yes," Joanne said. "This is exactly the kind of place Rod would have loved."

Eddie leaned close to me and said in my ear, "Don't let her go in the bedroom."

"You've been in here already?"

"I needed to check for damage."

Manny became restless in his father's arms. Now it made even less sense that he'd come with us. Maybe he'd only come to tell us about Rod's being behind on his rent. Aside from that, I wasn't sure if he should have come into the apartment alone. Technically, a landlord shouldn't enter without twenty-four hours' notice. Yes, his tenant was gone, but maybe his mother immediately became—

Joanne started toward the bedroom.

"Oh, Joanne, why don't you let my mom and I go in there first?"

"Why shouldn't I go into my son's—" And then her face blanched as she seemed to realize he'd died in there. "Oh, you don't have to. I'll probably sleep on the sofa anyway."

"Don't worry about a thing, Joanne," my mother said. "That's why we're here."

As my mother and I walked into the bedroom I heard Eddie saying, "I should get back to the kids and this one wants his cookie. Again, I'm sorry about Rod."

"Thank you."

The bedroom was very large with the same cathedral ceiling. To our right when we walked in was a small bathroom, to our left a wall of closets. He'd spent less money on this room, the only furniture being a queen-sized bed with a black lacquer headboard and two matching nightstands. Above the bed was a framed Herb Ritts poster of two naked bodybuilders wrapped around each other, their bodies taking on an abstract, almost geographic quality.

The sheets and blanket were messy. One of the pillows was on the floor. The bedding was light gray and when I got closer I saw that it was soiled. Quickly, I stripped everything off so Joanne wouldn't have to see the indignity of her son's last moments. I opened the large closet and found a wicker hamper. I put the sheets and a thin blanket in there with Rod's dirty clothes. I started to put the hamper back into the closet, but realized I couldn't leave this laundry for Joanne to do.

"We have to do the laundry," I said.

"Do you see another set of sheets in the closet?"

"No."

"Oh, here's a linen closet in the bathroom."

My mother stepped into the bathroom. I noticed there was an ivory box on one of the nightstands. I realized what might be in there and went over. Lifting the lid, I saw I was right: I found condoms, a small bottle of lube and a cock ring. That made me realize there was more to be dealt with than just the bedding.

Typically when a gay man dies, a friend or friends rush to get into his apartment first and remove anything that might embarrass his family: magazines, videos, lubes, condoms, drug stashes, sex toys. Robert was the one to do it for Jeffer. I imagined that Louis and Marc might someday do it for me. Rod, unfortunately, didn't have any friends hanging around trying to spare his mother embarrassment. That left it up to me.

My mother came out of the bathroom with a set of red satin sheets. "These must be for special occasions." I wasn't sure what kind of special occasion she was thinking of so I let it pass.

"You have to get Joanne out of here. I need to go through the entire apartment," I said quietly.

She set the sheets on the bed and began putting the pillows into their cases. "Are you looking for evidence? I thought you disagreed that it was—"

"No, I'm looking for things that would be…embarrassing. To Joanne."

She looked at me a moment and then said, "Oh. Yes, of course." She leaned forward and whispered, "I know what men are like. Your father kept girlie magazines in his tool box."

"I really didn't want to know that."

Shaking out the bottom sheet, she continued, "Of course, I found them long before he died. I didn't say anything. That would have been truly embarrassing. It did explain why he was sometimes, well, friendly when he came up from the basement."

"Oh God. Look, I need quarters for the laundry. Take Joanne with you and go down to the Mayfair on Franklin."

"But I have a roll of quarters in my purse. Isn't that enough?"

We'd gotten the bottom sheet on and were now stretching out the top sheet. The sheets were kind of slippery and I wondered if anyone had ever fallen off.

"Mom, why are you walking around with so many quarters?"

"Parking meters." She'd come prepared.

"Okay, well, take Joanne to get more."

"But we don't need more. Do we? I'm sure I have plenty."

"It's an excuse."

"Why don't we use a different excuse, though? A more productive one."

It didn't really make any difference. "All right. What do you want to tell her?"

"Oh. I'm not sure. What else do we need?" She finished tucking in the top sheet and stood up. "Food."

"What about it?"

"She'll need food. I'm sure there's nothing here. We'll just go grocery shopping." And with that she walked out into the living room. I followed close behind.

"Joanne, I'm thinking—"

My mother stopped when she saw the look on Joanne's face. She sat at the desk. In her lap was an open file of what looked like bank statements.

"There's no money," she said. "He told me he'd always take care of me, but there's no money."

"We don't need to think about that right now," my mother said. "There's no food in the house, Joanne. Why don't we run out and get a few things?"

"Oh, I don't know."

"I insist. Noah, is there someplace we can walk to?"

"No, take my car." I went back into the living room and reached into my jeans for the keys.

"Oh, no dear, I can't drive in L.A."

"You're not getting on the freeway. You're just going south to Franklin and turning left. There's a Mayfair a few blocks down. It's kitty-corner from the Scientology center."

"The what?"

"You'll see it. Big mansion. Religious zealots on the lawn."

"Which way is south?"

I pointed. She gave me a doubtful look.

"All right. Joanne, we should go—"

"I don't know what to do first."

"First, we're going to get you some food. You have to keep up your strength."

My mother dug into her purse, and before she led Joanne out of the apartment handed me the roll of quarters. Mentally, I crossed my fingers hoping that they—and my car—came back in one piece. Then I went back into the bedroom.

It wasn't obvious, but the police had rifled through everything. The drawers of the nightstands were ajar, as were several of the drawers on the tall dresser I discovered in the closet. The mattress sat askew on top of the box spring—something I should have noticed when we were making the bed. I looked into the drawer of the nightstand on the left side of the bed. More condoms, a different kind of lube and a small bottle of poppers. I wondered if Rod's sex life was really that active or if he was just the over-prepared sort.

I glanced at the expiration date on the condoms. His had quite a while left before they expired, which made me a little jealous. I'd just thrown away a whole box of expired condoms. I mean, I could have found someone to use them with, it's just that it was all so complicated now. And I wanted to avoid complicated.

Going over to the closet, I looked at the dresser inside. It had three drawers. Starting at the top: socks, underwear—heavy on the Calvin Klein, next, T-shirts, and then random miscellaneous things, including ties, pajamas, Speedos, a sweater vest and an uncomfortably large pink dildo. The dildo went right into the bag.

I ran my hand across the shelf above Rod's clothes—a lot of clothes, obviously expensive—and didn't find what I was looking for. Magazines. But guys didn't "read" porno magazines the way they used to—or the way my father apparently had. I remembered all too clearly going into Walgreens when I was a teenager and working up the nerve to buy *Playgirl*. Apparently, I looked humiliated and embarrassed by the purchase, because the clerk said to me, "Next time, make your mother or your older sister or whoever made you do this buy it themselves."

No, these days, everyone got their porn on VHS. Which reminded me; I went out into the living room and looked through the TV stand: *Star Wars*, *Indiana Jones and the Temple of Doom*, *Top Gun*, *E.T. the Extraterrestrial*. And, bingo, *Chi Chi LaRue's the Rise*. That last one went right into the Bullock's bag.

Then I went into the bathroom and opened up the medicine cabinet. There wasn't much in there except some allergy medicines, Tylenol, a half a bottle of Nyquil, and more than a dozen bottles of vitamins—A through zinc. I wondered if he took them all the time or had taken them once and then ignored them.

I went into the living room and sat down at his desk for a moment. Next to the Macintosh portable computer was a thick blue book, *A Course in Miracles*. I picked it up and leafed through it. It was pretty obviously not a book about witches and warlocks—as I'd half hoped. It looked vaguely religious. It was also the only book I'd seen in Rod's apartment. I was not a big reader either, but if I was going to start I don't think I'd start with *A Course in Miracles*. It looked dense.

I opened each of the drawers in the file cabinets that held up the desk. There were files hanging in Pendaflex folders. There might be embarrassing things in there, but I didn't have enough time to check. Standing up, I scanned the living room. I didn't see anywhere else where things could be hidden. Not expecting to find anything, I went into the kitchen and opened a few cupboards. I opened the fridge and found more vitamins. That seemed strange. No one needed this many vitamins, so why did he have them?

It would be a while before my mother and Joanne came back. Since I was finished with my search, I decided to put the laundry in so Joanne wouldn't have to. I also needed to throw away the bag of Rod's goodies. I grabbed what I needed and left the apartment.

I walked down the stairs to the courtyard, around the pool and then up past Eddie's building. As I did, I could hear a child crying, or maybe it was two. Clearly, he had his hands full just then.

I kept going toward the back of the building, keeping an eye out for the laundry room. I finally found it behind the building. Just beyond, I saw the dumpster for the complex set inside a metal gate. I tossed Rod's goodies into the dumpster, then went into the laundry room. No one else was doing laundry; not surprising on the day after a holiday.

As carefully as possible, I put the sheets into the washer, not wanting to touch them. Then I started putting in Rod's clothes. I took a pair of jeans out of the basket and stuck my hands in the pockets to make sure they were empty. That netted me three more quarters and a creased business card for someone named C.B.; just C.B. Below the initials were the words Live, Laugh, Love. And then a phone number. Maybe it wasn't a 'business' card; maybe it was a kind of personal card—though I didn't know many people who carried those. I shrugged and slipped the card into my pocket with the remaining quarters, and threw the jeans into the washing machine.

I went back up to Rod's apartment. It wouldn't be much longer until my mother and Joanne came back. I decided to check out the balcony. Actually, deck was a better description. It was too big for a balcony. And the roof below was covered in wooden decking, so it was definitely a deck.

Outside, I found there were bamboo screens on one side to block off the neighbors and a wooden railing running around the entire deck. On the right side was something I hadn't noticed before: There was a flight of stairs running along the side of the building from the courtyard to the street. There was also an opening in the deck's railing and a short flight of stairs that ran down to the courtyard level. Once there, you could either go out into the courtyard or take the stairs down to the street where there was a locked security door.

It did occur to me that Rod's apartment wasn't very secure. Anyone in the building could have come up to his deck. And if he left the sliding doors unlocked, they could walk right in. Of course, that didn't change anything. It was still unlikely he was murdered.

There was a round metal-and-glass table with an umbrella

and matching chairs sitting right outside the sliding doors. On the far side of the deck was a single lounge chair. That seemed redundant since there were a whole lot of them next to the pool. Maybe this one was for more private sunbathing. I mean, no one could see Rod up here. Well, there was a building across the street, but they'd have to make an effort. And not everyone would mind if an attractive young man slipped out of his bathing suit on his private deck.

I was about to go out to the edge and take a good look at the view when I heard a woman's voice next door to my left. Number 16. Tabitha, the awful neighbor.

"Where did he go to?" she asked.

"He's up at the laundry. I saw him walk up there with Rod's hamper." That was her husband, Allan. Apparently he hadn't seen me come back.

"He's doing laundry? Why is *he* doing laundry?"

The wind picked up and I didn't hear Allan's answer. Instead, I heard Tabitha ask, "Where did the old ladies go?"

"I don't know. It's not like I can yell out the window and ask."

"The Kileys aren't going to be happy about the mother showing up." I stepped over to the bamboo and squinted. I couldn't see much more than a patch of skin. "How long do you think she's staying?"

"Rod didn't say she was coming. I would have said something if I'd known," Allan said. He seemed like the whiny sort.

"I guess it doesn't matter. We get paid either way."

"Are we still going to Hawaii?"

"No. I'm thinking Belize."

"As long as there's a beach, I'm on it."

Behind me I heard my mother and Joanne come into the apartment. They had a half dozen white plastic bags filled with groceries. As quietly as I could, I tip-toed back over to the slider and slid the screen open without making any noise. I raised a finger to my mouth to let my mother know not to say anything. She looked at me funny but kept her mouth shut.

I stepped into the apartment and slid the glass door shut

behind me. In a low voice, I said, "Tabitha and Allan are out on the deck. They've been keeping track of everything we're doing."

"Oh dear," my mother said.

"They're not happy about Joanne showing up."

"What business is it of theirs?" Joanne asked. She and my mother had walked over to the dining table and set their bags on it. They began sorting out their purchases. It looked like Joanne had a penchant for junk food.

"We only got as far as the 7-Eleven," my mother explained.

"I'm not interested in cooking right now," Joanne said.

I guess that's understandable, though I didn't see how Cheetos, Slim Jims and Dr. Pepper were going to keep her going. I was tempted to relay the rest of the conversation I'd overheard, but I wasn't sure what it meant. The Kileys paid them or were paying them. Enough to go on a nice vacation. So, what had the Kileys paid them to do? I had no idea.

Of course I rushed to the idea that they might have been paid to kill Rod. But for the price of a vacation? That seemed awfully cheap. Even for a nice vacation. Though, I had no idea what the going rate for murder was. Or why the Kileys would want Rod dead. Or even who they were.

"Are you sure you want to stay here, Joanne?" I asked.

"Oh yes. I can feel Rod all around me."

"But, you think someone murdered him."

"Yes, I do."

"So what if—"

"Oh don't be silly," she cut me off. "The only reason anyone would kill my son would be jealousy. I'm sure some rejected lover couldn't stand seeing him with anyone else. I suppose that's romantic in a way."

"I'm sure there are other possible reasons," I said.

"Well he certainly wasn't killed for his money since it's—oh, that reminds me. There was somewhere else I wanted to look—"

She stopped unpacking groceries and went over to the desk. Sitting down, she opened one of the file drawers and flipped through. "Here, this. This is it." She pulled out a file and opened it on her lap. Flipping through a couple of sheets of paper, she found the one she wanted. She read for a moment, then pressed the entire file to her heart.

"I knew it. He promised he'd always take care of me. He wouldn't lie about something like that." She smiled at us, bit her lip and said, "He has an insurance policy."

7

"You realize this is kind of insane," I said, turning onto Franklin.

"What is, dear?"

"Well, we're driving back to Silver Lake and then back to Hollywood, then to wherever Scottie lives and then back to Silver Lake again." Before we left, we'd agreed to come back and take Joanne to see Rod's ex-lover, Scottie. "We're going to spend half the day driving."

"Good. Then I'll get to feel like a real Los Angeleno."

"No, just Angeleno."

"Angeleno. Thank you." She looked out the window, intently studying the buildings as we passed by them.

"Didn't you think it was weird the way Joanne acted about Rod's insurance?"

"You mean because the money is so important to her?"

"Yeah, I guess."

"Well, it is all she has left of him. And she does have other children to think about. And grandchildren." Looking out the window, she switched topics. "I think the architecture is so interesting out here. I just love these old Spanish buildings."

It didn't seem like Joanne was thinking about her other kids, though. It seemed like she was thinking about the money. And about her having the money. She'd been very excited when she showed us her name on the beneficiary line.

"Apparently, he promised to take care of her. Which is an easy thing to say but a much harder thing to do."

"Mom, I didn't tell Joanne everything I heard the neighbors say. I was afraid of frightening her."

She stopped looking out the window and turned her full attention on me. "Now you're frightening me. What did they say?"

"Allan mentioned people called the Kileys who are paying them enough to go on vacation in Belize."

"To do what?"

"I don't know, but it has something to do with Rod."

"Oh, you should have said something to Joanne. Maybe these Kileys are people she knows."

"She hasn't mentioned anyone like that, has she?"

"Like what? We just know their name."

"No, we know that they have money. And they're willing to pay Tabitha and Allan to do…something."

"Maybe they were just watching Rod for the Kileys?"

"But why would they be doing that?"

"I don't know." She took in the scenery for a moment, then asked, "Do you think it's drugs? They could be watching to see when he takes delivery."

I glanced over at her. Clearly she was watching too much TV.

"What?" she asked.

"Nothing. I don't think it's drugs. It looks like Rod likes his pot, but if he was dealing I think he'd have a lot more money in the bank. Or under the mattress."

"We didn't look under the mattress."

"I'm pretty sure the police did." Suddenly, I had a thought. "Maybe that's it."

"What's it?"

"Maybe he owes the Kileys money and that's why the neighbors were watching him. And what are the Kileys anyway? Are they a family? A boy band? The Irish Mafia?"

"I don't know," my mother said. "But we have to convince Joanne not to stay there. She may not be safe."

"I think you're right."

At about five after eleven we pulled up in front of Pinx Video. My store was on Hyperion wedged between a dry cleaner and a Taco Maria. Plate glass windows ran across the front of the building and were filled with posters from current and upcoming videos. The building was painted a dusty blue.

That Wednesday I'd cleaned the windows myself and swept the sidewalk out front. Two days later you could barely tell I'd done a thing. Hopefully, my mother wouldn't notice.

We walked in. The store is pretty simple: shelves with video boxes on one side, a rental counter in the middle, and a room behind the counter where we kept the actual videos in black and brown plastic boxes. My tiny office was in the back.

Behind the counter was my employee Mikey Kellerman. In his mid-thirties, Mikey was thin and balding. He liked to be in charge, so he was going to be thrilled when I told him I'd be out most of the weekend.

"Mikey, this is my mother."

"Oh, it's nice to meet you Mrs. Valentine."

"Angie."

"Angie. How is your visit going? Are you enjoying Los Angeles?"

"Well—"

"It's been eventful," I said, not wanting to get into it.

"Um, all right," Mikey said.

Before he could say anything else, I asked, "So, do you know anything about a movie called *They Come at Night?* It's from Monumental."

"Of course. We have two copies of it."

"We do?"

"It came out in January and it has that actress Monica Blaine."

"The one that was caught skinny dipping with her married director?" my mother said. She loved movie gossip.

"That's the one."

"Those pictures," she clucked, referring to some pictures that appeared in the *National Inquisitor*.

"You'll see even more of her in this movie."

"Oh, I don't think so."

"The script coordinator, we know his mother."

"He died," my mother said.

"Oh really? Recently?"

"Wednesday night. Drug overdose."

"You know, I've heard Monica Blaine has a little problem in that area."

"Really? She's such a pretty girl. It would be a shame to ruin that."

"So," I interrupted. "Could you look up Rod Brusco and see if he's one of our clients?"

Mikey hit a few key strokes and then asked, "On Cahuenga Boulevard?"

"That's him, yes. When was the last time he was in?"

"About six months ago. He rented *They Come at Night* and *The Bigger the Better*."

"*The Bigger the Better*?" my mother said. "I missed that one."

I leaned over and said softly, "It's a porno."

"Oh, well, I guess that's why I missed it."

"He brought it back late," Mikey said. "Almost a week."

That was no surprise. Rod didn't seem to have been the most organized person in the world.

"You know, I think I remember him," Mikey said. "He didn't want to pay his late fee. We had a big argument about it and then you came out and waived his late fees."

"I did?"

"Yes, you did," Mikey said. By the look on his face I could tell he was still annoyed by it. "I think he was faking it, too. Kept saying he'd had to have medical services."

A customer, an older man in a stained shirt, rushed into the store and hurried over to the counter. He set a couple of videos in our branded plastic bag onto the counter then hurried back out. I couldn't help but frown. My business model was based on customers picking out a new video or two every time they came to return one. That way I was renting to them twice a week. Sometimes more.

"What's your favorite video, Mikey?" my mother asked.

"Oh, I couldn't pick a favorite. I mean, it depends on what genre and what mood I'm in."

"Well, what do you recommend? If we're going to take one home tonight, what would you suggest?"

"I would suggest *Tootsie* on laserdisc, but certain people don't have a laserdisc player."

"I have a thirteen-inch television, as you well know. Hooking a laserdisc player to that makes about as much sense as having Francis Ford Coppola direct *Police Academy 7*."

Mikey shivered at the thought. "In that case, a copy of *Sister Act* just came in. You could have that."

"Mom, we're going to dinner."

"This would be for after."

"Aren't you exhausted? You were up most of Wednesday night and you couldn't have slept well last night."

I was exhausted. And I hadn't slept well. I was ashamed to admit it, but I was already looking forward to Monday night after I put her on the plane.

Mikey decided not to wait for our decision. He pulled the tape out of a stack he hadn't put away yet, then turned to the computer screen to check it out to me. Before he finished, I said "Why don't you give me *They Came at Night* too."

You never know.

"I'm not tired all," my mother said. "It must be the excitement."

"Are you getting hungry?"

"Oh yes, I need more than a slice of pie to go all day. Though it was really delicious." She turned to Mikey and said, "Noah's friend Louis made the cleverest pumpkin pie. Just delicious."

"You know, we could go to Taco Maria's, but I was thinking of La Casita Grande for dinner tonight."

"That's fine."

"What's fine? You want Mexican twice in one day?"

"Mexicans eat Mexican food at every meal." That was true, though I doubted they called it Mexican food. In Mexico it was just food. "Are they fast? Or should we get it to go?"

"You mean, eat when we get back to Rod's apartment?"

"Or in the car. That's a very L.A. thing to do, isn't it?"

I had to admit it was. Putting makeup on while driving was also a very L.A. thing to do, though I didn't recommend it. In the end, we got four chicken tacos and ate them in the car while sharing a gigantic root beer. I have to say, it was kind of fun.

LUCKILY, Scottie only lived about a half mile from The Pagoda, though it was a bit of a challenge to drive to. The condominium complex clung to the side of a hill on the west side of the Cahuenga Pass overlooking the 405. So we had to find the entrance on Cahuenga Boulevard West which was on the opposite side of the 405. We missed our first chance to cross over from Cahuenga Boulevard East and had to drive almost into Studio City to get another.

When we finally made it to the condominium complex, we found a virtual forest of trees in front meant to mask the constant whoosh of passing traffic. They didn't. The complex itself was dozens of cubes stuck together in seemingly random ways. Really, the place looked like a giant baby had been playing with blocks in the woods and then abandoned them when something more interesting presented itself.

Before we could get to Scottie's front door, it popped open and out he came. "Joanne! It's so lovely to see you!" He scooped her up and squeezed her. He was not what I'd been expecting. I'd been expecting your basic West Hollywood circuit boy, but Scottie was tall, wide and bearded. He wore a Tom of Finland T-shirt with a hairy, thickly muscled guy in a jock strap. The model was not unlike Scottie.

He let go of Joanne and said the oddest thing, "Where's Rod? When you said you wanted to come over, I assumed…"

"Scottie, the worst has happened. Our boy is gone!"

"Gone? You mean he's run away?" He had a soft Southern accent that increased as he became upset. "I can't say I'm surp—"

Joanne shook her head.

"Oh. Oh my. How? When?"

"Wednesday night. They're saying he overdosed, but that—"

"He wouldn't have," Scottie said. "He wasn't doing any drugs. Well, I mean, other than marijuana. And you can't over-dose on—I'm so sorry, y'all should come in."

He led the way into the small but attractive condominium. It was a great place, though it was unfortunate that even with the windows shut you could hear the traffic from the eight lanes of the 101 freeway below us. The first thing I noticed about Scottie's living room was that it wasn't entirely furnished. There was a leather occasional chair that matched the one at Rod's and a glass end table, but the other furniture was a canvas lounge chair and a cast iron settee, both of which belonged on the now empty balcony.

"Oh, Scottie, Rod has your furniture doesn't he? You can have it back if you want."

"Thank you, Joanne. The furniture was his, but I won't say no to a comfortable place to sit." He stopped and took a deep breath. "Oh my God, poor Rod. My head is spinning. I'm not sure I really believe it."

Joanne sat down in the leather chair. It was becoming obvious she wasn't going to introduce us, so I asked, "How long were you and Rod together?"

"Oh! I'm sorry," Joanne said. "Scottie, this is Noah and his mother, Angie."

We said hello and shook Scottie's hand. He invited us to sit down, so we sat on the very uncomfortable cast iron settee. Then Joanne told Scottie the story of how she and my mother met and figured out they both had gay sons. It was already taking on the quality of a family myth.

"So you've been taking care of Joanne? That's so nice of y'all."

"It hasn't been a problem," I said. I could have added that it had been a lot of driving. And luggage carrying. "So, how long were you and Rod together?"

"About a year and a half. He and I, we just grew apart." He got a faraway look, which might have been him remembering again that Rod was gone or he might have been thinking about their breakup, which probably wasn't as amicable as he said. I'm sure there was a couple somewhere who really did 'just grow apart,' but for most people that expression meant they didn't want to talk about the breakup.

"But you stayed friends," Joanne said. "Rod told me how important that was to him."

Scottie's smile was a bit strained, but he said, "We did."

"Did he talk much about his neighbors, Tabitha and Allan?" I asked.

"He did for a while. When he moved in he thought they were wonderful. Then he stopped talking about them."

"We're pretty sure he went to a party at their apartment Wednesday night."

"He did like a party. Do you think they had something to do with his dying?"

"Probably not," I said.

"I think so," Joanne disagreed. To Scottie she added, "They're acting very shifty."

I asked, "Did Rod mention any of his other neighbors?"

"Actually, he had something to say about most of them. Let's see, one of them was a jealous maniac. I think he lives in number 6?"

"We met the guy in number 5. He mentioned Rod trying to take his boyfriend."

"That's probably him. But *take* is the wrong word. Borrow perhaps, but never take."

"Rod was always such a flirt," his mother said, as though borrowing boyfriends was form of clever repartee.

"The people downstairs complained about noise a few times. But Rod had the owner of the building wrapped around his little finger."

"Really? How so?"

"I don't know, he never made that clear. But Rod could charm the birds from the sky."

"Oh he could, he could."

"And then again, he might have been telling tales."

Then I asked, "Did he ever mention anyone named Kiley?"

"Hmmm, no, I don't think so."

"Who is that?" Joanne asked.

"It's just something I overheard. I don't know what it means."

"It might mean nothing," my mother said.

"What am I thinking? I haven't offered you all a thing. Joanne, coffee?"

"With bourbon?"

"I haven't forgotten, darlin'."

"Just coffee," I said.

"Yes, coffee, please," my mother said.

As he left the room, Scottie caught my eye and made a motion for me to follow.

"I should probably help," I said, getting up before anyone could say anything. I doubted Scottie needed help making coffee. Few people did.

The kitchen was a small, square room with a swinging door. That would probably be annoying a lot of the time, but right now it was a godsend.

"Listen dear, there's a lot I don't want to say in front of Joanne."

That was surprising since he'd already said a lot. Still, I agreed. "I know. I went through Rod's apartment and got rid of the, you know, gay stuff before she saw it."

"Oh, thank you. That was so kind of you."

I shrugged. "So, you know more about his next door neighbors, don't you?"

"I'm fairly certain he had sex with the stripper. He had this way of talking about his conquests that was unmistakable." Standing at the sink, he poured water into the coffee carafe. "I mean, he never said exactly, but there would be a change in the way he said a man's name."

"So Tabitha might have been jealous?" I suggested.

"Oh, I suppose."

"You mean you're not sure if she was jealous?"

"Rod said she was into the idea of her husband with other men."

"So do you think the three of them—?"

"Oh, who knows! That boy. I think he'd try anything once. Or twice. Or until he got bored." He poured the water from the carafe into the machine and then took out the coffee basket.

"Is that why you broke up? Because Rod wasn't faithful?"

"Oh, I couldn't care less about that. No, Rod and I broke up because of the money."

"What do you mean 'because of the money'? Because he ran out of it?"

After he slipped a paper filter into the basket, he scooped coffee grounds from a can into the basket. "There's a bottle of bourbon in that cupboard, could you grab it?"

I did as I was asked. Then I waited for him to answer my question.

"No, it wasn't because he ran out of money, although that was certainly inconvenient. It was because he kept lying about it. At first he said it came from an old boyfriend, but I could never nail down which one. Then he said it was some kind of settlement and he couldn't legally talk about it. I might have believed that one if he hadn't told me the three other lies first."

Scottie turned on the coffeemaker and it began to steam. Then he went to the refrigerator and took out a pint carton of hazelnut creamer.

"So you have no idea where the money came from?"

"None. All I know about the money is that it's gone. Spent. Every last penny."

He found a tray in a cabinet and then pulled down four cups from a cupboard.

"How did the two of you meet?" I asked.

"I used to work at the French Market as a second job on the weekends. Used to, ha! I'll be starting there again in about a month. Rod was in Best Lives. They meet at West Hollywood

Universal Church. They'd come in afterwards in groups of five or ten. I waited on him two or three times and then he asked if he could buy me a drink and, you know, one thing led to another."

"What is Best Lives?" I naively asked.

"Oh, you haven't heard of them? They're a group for HIV positive men."

"Oh, that's right, I forgot." I hadn't exactly forgotten. I knew there were groups out there like that. I just hadn't learned their names, hadn't wanted to. "Wait. Are you saying Rod was positive?"

"Yes."

"No," I said, a gut reaction. "There weren't any, um, medications in his apartment. No AZT. No Bactrim. All I found was vitamins."

Scottie rolled his eyes. "That boy." He looked me over, sizing me up, and said, "If you don't know Best Lives then you probably don't know there are a lot of people out there who won't take AZT. They call it poison. Rod was following a strict detoxification diet, exercising and taking vitamins by the truckload."

He was right. I didn't know much about this. There had been some articles in *LA Weekly*, but I hadn't wanted to do more than skim them. If AZT didn't work, I really didn't want to know.

"That's all? That's all he was doing?"

"Oh, and *A Course in Miracles.*"

"I saw that book. What is it, exactly?"

"Oh God, I have been to lectures, I have read and read and read and darlin' I still have no idea what that book is about. It has something to do with life not being real and we're just making all of this up as we go along so we can change it if we want to. Of course, if you've ever truly tried to change your life you'd know what a crock that is."

That would appeal to someone who thought he was dying of AIDS, I suppose. The idea that he could think his way out of a disease. I'd certainly like to be able to think my way out of it.

Then something occurred to me. "His health was good? I mean, he wouldn't have deliberately—"

"His health was very good. Honestly, I don't know why. I think what he was doing was crazy. But, well, there's a lot to be said for belief. He believed the things he was doing would make him well and they did. I think they call it a placebo effect."

He took the carafe out of the coffeemaker and poured four cups.

"Does Joanne know he was HIV positive?" I asked.

He shook his head. "I don't think so. He'd hate it if she did."

I nodded.

Then Scottie and I carried the coffee out to the living room —well, Scottie carried it; I just walked behind him carrying the bourbon. Once everyone had their cup, he poured generous shots into his and Joanne's. The two of them began to reminisce about poor Rod. Most of the stories were about Rod doing terrible things and getting out of trouble by smiling or telling a joke.

In one story, he tried to get revenge on a terrible boss by putting the woman's garden hose through an open window in her living room and then turning it on. The LAPD patrol officer who caught him at it decided to let him go after forty minutes of stories about how hideously the woman treated her employees, some of which were even true.

More bourbon was poured and more stories told, then it was nearly two-thirty. We only had a bit more than an hour to take Joanne home, convince her she shouldn't stay there, drive to my apartment, and drop my mother and Joanne off in time for me to leave for my meeting with Javier.

When I brought up the time, Joanne said, "Why don't you just leave me here. Scottie can bring me back to Rod's, can't you dear?"

"I sure can, darlin'."

I glanced at my mother. This was unexpected.

"The thing is, Joanne," she said. "We were going to talk to you about something."

"You can talk in front of Scottie, he's like family."

"Well, we're not entirely sure you'll be safe there."

"Oh, don't be ridiculous."

"But Joanne," I said. "You've said yourself you think that Rod was murdered. Aren't you in danger staying in his apartment? I mean the next door neighbors—"

"Relax, I'm just fine." She picked up her purse off the floor next to her chair and put it on her lap. She rifled through it, saying, "If they try anything I'm completely prepared." Then she pulled a pistol out of her purse. It was black with a pearl grip.

"Oh my God," my mother said.

"Where did that come from?" I asked.

"I brought it from South Bend. My grandson gave it to me."

"How did you get it on the plane?"

"You can always travel with a gun. You just put it in your suitcase. As long as you don't bring it on the plane with you, they don't care."

That was not a terribly reassuring thought.

"Now, where are those bullets? If I'm in danger I should probably load the damned thing."

"Joanne, even with the gun…" my mother said.

"If anyone tries to mess with me I'll drop them cold. I'm a very good shot."

"She is," Scottie agreed.

I didn't ask how he knew that.

8

My mother stared me down as we sat in my car outside my apartment. "I'm not going in until you tell me what you and Scottie talked about in the kitchen."

I'd been hoping to keep that information to myself, at least until dinner. I wanted some time to decide whether it meant anything. If it didn't mean anything then I couldn't see a reason to tell everyone. And I was especially concerned that if I told everyone it would get back to Joanne.

Unfortunately, my mother was not going to let me off the hook.

"Joanne doesn't know this but Rod was HIV positive."

"Oh, I see."

"He was treating it with vitamins, exercise and positive thinking."

"Oh my Lord. You wouldn't consider that would you? I mean, you're on medication. I saw you take it at lunch."

Actually, she'd helped me. Juggling a taco, a root beer and AZT while driving across L.A. is practically a circus act.

"No, no. I'm fine with what I'm doing. I mean, taking some vitamins probably wouldn't hurt me, but I'm not going to take them instead."

"It must be terrifying for you," she said softly.

This was a road I did not want to go down. "Mom, I'm going to be late."

"All right, all right." She took off her safety belt, leaned in and kissed me on the cheek. "I have the key," she said, holding up the spare key to my apartment.

"Take a nap. I'll be back in an hour."

"Oh I couldn't possibly sleep. Not after a day like today. I've got these movies," she said, holding up the bag. "I might start one without you."

"All right," I said, though I'd have preferred she napped.

She got out of the car and I watched as she climbed up the red steps. Then I took Maltman up and over to Sunset. There, on the far side of the street, was the coffee house where I'd be meeting Detective Javier O'Shea.

The Living Room was located in a storefront and did its best to live up to its name with Persian rugs, mismatched sagging sofas and well-used chairs. Bookcases full of used books lined the walls. There was a clock over the counter and I noticed I was five minutes late.

I looked around and found Javier sitting in a wingback chair. I felt a little pang. I hadn't seen him in a long time and had done a good job of forgetting exactly how good-looking he was. Black hair, sandy eyes, caramel skin, strong jaw—God, I was a little weak in the knees just looking at him.

"Hi," I said, sitting down across from him.

"Get yourself a coffee and come back."

"That's okay. I don't really…I mean…um. Hi."

He gave me a funny look, probably because I was acting like an idiot. He got down to business.

"Rod Brusco died between midnight and 3 a.m. Thursday morning."

"Oh, okay. So the party might have still been going on next door."

"Possibly. I only have the autopsy. At the moment, the cause of death is undetermined. The coroner has concerns."

"He does? Really?" I told myself to behave less like a

96

teenaged girl, but I didn't exactly listen. "Um, it's really nice to see you."

"Uh-huh," he said. It was a dismissive sound. "The coroner won't make a final determination for four to six weeks. After the tox screen comes back."

"Wait, the tox screen—toxicology?"

He nodded. I wondered why he was being so formal. But that was stupid. He was being formal because I'd hurt him. It wasn't that hard to figure out. I decided it was best to follow his lead and be formal too.

"That takes four to six weeks? Is that standard?" I asked.

"Yes."

"So you knew this morning that you weren't going to be able to get me a definitive answer." He could have told me all this over the phone. We didn't have to meet. But then, the way he was behaving, this wasn't making sense.

"That's not entirely true," he explained. "The coroner might have found that he was killed in some other way."

"Oh. But he didn't find that. Did he?"

"He found things that concern him."

"Like?"

"Rod's eyes were badly bloodshot. That might be because he smoked a lot of marijuana. And there was marijuana in the apartment. The tox screen—"

"Or?" He wouldn't be talking about this if there wasn't a more sinister possibility.

"Or bloodshot eyes can be an indication that a person has been suffocated or strangled."

"Is that the only concerning thing?"

"There was some light bruising on his face. The preliminary report suggests he was at a party, so he might have been in a fight. Someone might have slapped him."

"Or?"

"Or something may have been pressed on his face."

"Like a pillow?"

"Yes. Like a pillow."

"Is that all?"

"There was no aspirated vomit in his lungs."

"And why is that important?"

"It's common in drug overdoses, though it doesn't happen every time."

"They took the marijuana out of his apartment. Did they find anything else?"

"I only spoke to my contact in the coroner's office. No other drugs are mentioned in their report. That doesn't mean they weren't there."

"Let's say there were syringes, wouldn't they be mentioned?"

He nodded. "Probably.

"So, did they find needle marks?" I threw in a little lingo, "Tracks?"

"No."

"So, if he did overdose it had to have been prescription—"

"No, you can smoke heroin," Javier said. "Or snort it."

"I didn't know that."

"I'm glad you didn't know that. He could have smoked a small amount of heroin but drunk a lot of alcohol. The combination is what's deadly."

"His mother said he'd stopped doing hard drugs."

"Isn't that what you'd tell your mother if you were a drug addict?" Honestly, if I was a drug addict the last thing I'd do would be to tell my mother anything.

Javier continued, "Look, he might have given it up and then hit it a little too hard when he picked it up again. It happens."

"But that doesn't explain his bloodshot eyes or the bruising."

"No, it doesn't. But like I said, there are other ways to explain those things. Look, you really shouldn't get involved with this."

I felt like he had to say that. I was pretty sure the LAPD motto was 'To protect and to serve and to tell you to butt out.'

"What do you think of Detective Amberson?" I asked.

"He's good. He'll make sense of this."

I could have told him about the things I'd heard Rod's neighbors say or that Rod was HIV positive or that he'd once had a mysterious fortune that was now gone—but I didn't. I was too distracted by his cold manner and without really thinking it through found myself saying, "I'm sorry. I know you… like me."

"Please don't. I'm seeing someone now. So there's no need."

"You have a boyfriend?"

"I do."

"Oh." I tried not to look surprised. "Well, congratulations."

I guess that explained a lot. It also made me feel bad, but that was dumb. I mean, I'd barely thought about Javier for weeks and when I did it was to remind myself I was glad I hadn't seen him. We couldn't be together. It wouldn't work. I knew some people managed to be together even though one person was positive and the other wasn't, but that seemed too hard. He'd just come out, after all. And I could see him taking his gay baby steps. Well, a few baby leaps and bounds, but the last thing he needed to do was jump into a relationship with someone who might not even be around in a few years.

And maybe that was why I couldn't let things progress with Javier. If things had progressed, then I'd have to think about what would happen if I got really sick. I'd have to think about what would happen if I were to die. Single, I didn't need to think about those things. And believe me, I tried not to.

"Noah?"

"I'm sorry?"

"I asked if you got everything you were looking for?"

"Yes, I suppose I did."

LA CASITA GRANDE, which translated to something like The Big Cottage, was once a grand old mansion. Now, it was cut into a series of small dining rooms, each painted a different bold color. We were seated in the Indigo Room at a round table for five. The room was narrow and long, leaving space for two more tables. I suspected it had once been a summer sleeping porch where cool breezes could sweep in and banish the heat of the day.

Leon had joined us and was somewhat annoyingly complaining about this day. "I don't know why I got the bright idea to go to the Beverly Center the day after Thanksgiving."

"Black Friday," Louis reminded him.

"That's right! Another Madison Avenue plot. Anyway, all I wanted to do was go to Bullock's and do a tiny bit of Christmas shopping for my favorite person in the whole wide world: me. But I swear I couldn't find a place to park. I mean, I could have valeted, but that's five dollars at least *plus* a tip. So if you're not careful, you've spent the cost of a silk tie on parking."

"A good silk tie is at least twenty bucks," Louis pointed out.

"Not on Black Friday! They were on sale. Two for twenty."

"So did you find a place to park?" my mother asked.

"I did, finally. On the first floor, literally miles from an elevator."

"And how many ties did you buy?"

"Four. And two dress shirts. And this snazzy little paisley vest that I can wear on Casual Fridays."

"Black Friday. Casual Friday. Will we eventually have a name for every Friday?" my mother asked just as the waiter arrived. He was a short Mexican man in his mid-fifties. I started to order a strawberry margarita, but he stopped me.

"Ladies first."

"Oh, sorry."

"Well, I'm from Michigan where they make cars, so I think I'll have the Cadillac margarita," my mother said.

"Excellent choice," the waiter said. To make me pay for my faux pas he took everyone else's order first. Marc and Louis both ordered frozen margaritas.

Leon said, "I'm not from Michigan, but I'll still have a Cadillac margarita."

Finally, the waiter allowed me to order my strawberry margarita. Before he left, Louis ordered guacamole and chips.

"Do you like guacamole, Angie?"

"I do. I haven't had it often. I think we've only been getting avocados for ten or twelve years. No one knew what to do with them when they first started showing up in the stores. I'm embarrassed to say this, but my neighbors put mayonnaise in guacamole."

We all cringed as I think she knew we would. To be honest, growing up there were few things we didn't add mayonnaise to.

"All right, I can't wait any longer," Marc said. "What happened with Detective Delicious?"

"Oh, please don't call him that," I said, meaning don't call him that in front of my mother.

"Is he really that good-looking?" she wanted to know.

"He is," Leon said. "And you can trust me. I'm a connoisseur."

"You've certainly done your share of sampling," Louis teased.

"And proud of it too."

"Guys!" Marc said. "None of this is answering my question. Noah, what did you find out from Detective O'Shea?"

"It's *possible* that Rod Brusco was murdered. They can't really be sure until the toxicology report comes back and they see what drugs were in his system."

"Was he a drug addict?" Leon asked. "I wanted to ask that yesterday but not in front of his mother."

"If he was, he wasn't injecting anything. There are no needle marks listed in the autopsy."

"So we really didn't learn anything at all," Marc said, clearly disappointed.

"I wouldn't say that," Leon disagreed. "It's possible Rod was murdered. We can't rule it out."

"And we can't rule it in," I said.

"What does Javier's gut say?"

"I didn't ask."

"For heaven's sake, why not?"

"It's not his case."

"Tell them about the neighbors," my mother said.

"That's not important," I said.

"What?" Leon demanded. "Don't hide evidence from us."

I relayed as much as I could remember about what I'd overheard. A busboy brought out our guacamole and chips. Louis chewed thoughtfully on a chip and then said, "So it's possible he was murdered and it's possible the neighbors had something to do with it."

"I wouldn't say possible," Leon said. "I'd say probable. Obviously his neighbors were paid to kill him. Right?"

"Shouldn't they get more than a beach vacation for murdering someone though?" I wondered.

"You don't know they're not getting more than that. Maybe they're putting the rest into a retirement fund," Leon said.

"And then there's the money," my mother said.

"What about it?"

"He seems to have had money for a while and then he ran out," I explained. "Nobody seems to know where the money came from."

"Joanne said he inherited money from a dear friend."

"His ex-boyfriend told me Rod said different things about where the money came from. First he tried to say it came from an old lover and then he said it was from a settlement."

"What kind of settlement?" Marc asked.

"I don't know."

The waiter was back with our margaritas. He set my mother's down first, then served the others, leaving mine for last. Apparently he was the sort to hold grudges.

"Would you like to order your dinners now?" he asked.

"Oh, I haven't even looked at the menu," my mother said.

The waiter nodded politely in her direction and left.

"Looks like you've made a conquest, Angie," Leon said.

"Oh stop." She took a sip of her margarita. "Mmmm, very good. You know, it could have been a lawsuit."

We looked at her blankly for a moment.

"The settlement. There's a woman at the end of my block who fell in the produce section of Meijer and she got a settlement of fifty thousand dollars. She can't talk about it."

"It sounds like she did though," Marc said.

"Well, yes, she has a rather big mouth. And a very bad hip."

"Is she the neighbor who puts mayonnaise in her

guacamole?" Leon asked. My mother giggled and waved him off.

"If it was a legal settlement, it would explain why he wasn't always truthful about it," Louis said.

"But a settlement for what?" I wondered. "Who did he sue?"

"And does it have anything to do with his death?" my mother added.

I took a big sip of my drink and then scooped up some guacamole with a chip.

"So now Joanne is staying at her son's apartment? Actually sleeping there? In the same bed?" Leon asked, clearly uncomfortable with the idea.

"I think she's going to sleep on the sofa," I said, which still sounded depressing.

"Do you think it's a good idea for her to stay there?" Marc wanted to know. "After what you said about the neighbors."

"We tried to talk her out of it," my mother said. "But she has a gun so she feels safe."

"A gun?"

"Yes," I said. "She showed it to us."

"It's actually quite an attractive little pistol," my mother said.

"Mom!"

"Well, it is."

"What is Rod's apartment like?" Louis asked.

"Expensive. The rent is probably two hundred more than ours and he has a lot of pricey furniture."

"He liked leather," my mother said.

"Furniture," I added to clarify.

"Ah," Louis said, smirking at the idea of my mother meaning that he was 'into' leather.

"If he was out of money what was he living on?" Leon wondered.

"I don't know. He didn't seem to be working. As far as I know, the last movie he worked on came out a year ago."

"Oh, it was dreadful," my mother said. "I watched some of it while you were gone. The funniest part was this dinner scene.

There were three people at a table and in one shot there were two candles in the middle and then in the next shot there were four and then one and two, then three. Then I started watching the wine glasses that magically refilled—"

"I think that was Rod's job. That's what a script coordinator does is watch for those things."

"Script supervisor," Leon corrected me. "But on a low budget film they're often one and the same."

"That probably explains why he wasn't working anymore," I said.

"I have a question," my mother said, abruptly. "Is this what you did the other times?"

"What other times?" I asked.

"The other times you got involved in murder."

"Noah doesn't just get involved in murder," Leon said. "He catches the killer."

"What? Really?"

"Wilma Wanderley's son almost shot him."

"You were almost—they didn't say a word about that in the newspaper."

"Oh God, that would have been awful," I said.

"That's not true," Marc pointed out. "The *National Inquisitor* called him the 'unidentified mystery man present at Albert Wanderly's capture.'"

"And that's as close as I want to get to being in the newspaper. Or shot."

The waiter was back again for our order. My mother was immediately flustered. "Start with someone else. I'll be ready by the time you get to me."

Louis ordered the combination plate and Marc asked for a carne asada. While Leon ordered, Louis leaned over to my mother and said, "Angie, you should try the chicken mole."

"Now what is that?"

"It's chicken in a chocolate sauce."

"That's doesn't sound—

"No, it doesn't. But it's delicious."

"Really?"

"Yes."

Skeptically, my mother ordered the chicken mole and I ordered carnitas. Once the waiter walked away, Louis said, "All right. Rod's next-door neighbors are the prime suspects. Who else wanted Rod dead?"

"Louis, it was probably an overdose," I said.

"I know, but let's pretend it wasn't."

I rolled my eyes. "Obviously there are the next-door neighbors," I said, "and whoever they're working for. If that's what's going on."

"There's the guy in Number 5 who didn't like him much. He said Rod tried to steal his boyfriend. Maybe he succeeded," Marc suggested.

"Scottie," my mother said. "His ex."

"Oh but, he seems nice," I said.

"He was nice. But we don't really know what happened in their relationship, do we?"

"I guess we don't." I looked at my mother in a new light. She was much more cynical than I'd ever thought.

"Whoever he sued is a possible suspect. Revenge," suggested Louis.

"Now wait a minute," Leon said. "There's something else we know. Whoever killed Rod had to be able to get into the apartment. They had to have a key."

"Or they could have climbed over the balcony."

"So really anyone on the second floor," said Marc.

"Or anyone at the party that night."

"Actually, anyone from anywhere," I said. "There's a stairway up to his deck. If he didn't lock the slider anyone could walk right in."

9

THE NEXT MORNING I HAD A POUNDING HANGOVER AND, as if that wasn't bad enough, my mother was cheery and spry. And I was sure she'd had at least one more margarita than I'd had.

Crawling off the sofa cushions, I went into the bathroom, brushed my teeth, got my meds. Then, as I was walking through the bedroom, I grabbed my jeans and changed out of the old gym shorts I'd slept in. For the moment, I kept on my well-worn *Les Misérables* T-shirt.

"What time is it?"

"It's nearly nine o'clock. It's about time you got up. Do you always sleep this late?"

"What's that I smell?"

"It's a chicken casserole for Joanne."

"Where did you get—food?"

"Oh, Louis took me to the Mercado. I love that place. We don't have anything like it in Grand Rapids, which is really a shame. They have a wonderful selection and the prices are so reasonable."

"Are you sure Joanne needs a casserole? Isn't she supposed to leave tomorrow?"

"I think that's out of the question. I doubt she'll have her son's body back. And I don't think she'll go home without it."

I blinked a few times to chase the sleep from my eyes, and as I did I noticed that the Hockney was back on the wall. My mother had found it in the closet and put it back up. I decided not to mention it.

"I made coffee," she said, going into the kitchen to get me a cup. "And I bought you a Mexican pastry. Louis told me what it's called, but I've forgotten already."

She brought out a cup of coffee and a giant sweetbread that I wanted nothing to do with. I sat down at the table. Taking a sip of my coffee, I asked, "What are we doing today?"

"I just called Joanne, but she's not answering. Maybe she's not an early riser either."

The tone of her voice made me ask, "Does that make you nervous, her not answering?"

"Yes and no. I don't think she should have stayed there. But she is a grown woman."

"A grown woman with a gun," I said, ripping off a piece of the pastry. "And if she's shot the neighbors it might be a while before she can come to the phone."

"Oh, that's true, isn't it?"

"Mom, look, Rod was out of money. He hadn't worked in ages, his health may not have been that great, he used to be a drug addict. It's not hard to understand why he might have gone back to it."

"So you do think it was an accidental overdose?"

"I do."

"Then we need to help Joanne understand that, don't we?"

I nodded, then said, "We can leave in a few minutes if you want."

"Have your breakfast first."

I shoved the piece of pastry into my mouth, took a couple sips of the coffee, and said, "Ready."

"Oh Noah," she said, frowning at me. "At least put on a hat."

"I WONDER how late Joanne stayed at Scottie's?" my mother asked as we climbed the front stairs of The Pagoda forty-five minutes later—she had convinced me to drink the rest of my coffee and take a shower. I carried the still-warm casserole in front of me with both hands.

"I don't know. They seemed very chummy."

"She might have just come back and gone right to sleep. And she probably drank a lot more than we did." And I was a wreck, so maybe it's not surprising Joanne didn't answer the phone.

In the lobby, my mother pressed the button beside Brusco. Then we waited. And waited. Nothing happened. She looked at me, worry on her face.

"Is there one that says manager?"

"No."

"Do you remember Eddie's last name?" I felt like I should remember it. He'd said it. I was pretty sure.

"I *did* know his name. Now you've knocked it out of my head."

"Press number five."

"Number five?"

"Yes, that's guy we met. Remember?"

"Oh him, yes." She pressed the button for number 5. Gilbert, presumably his last name. I really wasn't sure he'd told us his name.

A few moments passed and then a voice came over the intercom, "Yeeeees?"

"Hi, we met yesterday. I'm hoping you can let us in," I said.

"I met a lot of people yesterday."

"We were wearing pajamas."

"Oh yes. The nosey ones."

"Rod's mother stayed here last night and now she's not answering the buzzer."

Suddenly, the door buzzed open. My mother and I walked around the courtyard and up the steps to number 17. I knocked on the door. Behind me my mother said, "Joanne? Joanne, wake up."

We waited. Nothing. Nothing but silence. This is what must have happened two mornings ago. Tabitha had stood here, knocking, waiting.

"Joanne!" my mother called out. "Joanne, please come to the door."

Then I heard the flap of flip-flops on the concrete. I turned and saw that Number 5 was coming toward us with Eddie behind him. Both were in shorts and flip-flops.

"Is she answering?" Number 5 asked.

We shook our heads.

"I grabbed Eddie. He's got a key."

"I called her earlier and she didn't answer. Now she's not coming to the door," my mother explained.

"You know, Mom, she might have just stayed with Scottie overnight."

Eddie opened the door and stepped into the apartment. "Mrs. Brusco? Mrs. Brusco, are you here?"

Stepping into the apartment behind Eddie, I saw Joanne lying peacefully on the sofa.

"Joanne? Joanne, wake-up."

My mother set the casserole down on the coffee table and went to the sofa. She nudged Joanne and then took her hand and rubbed it. "Joanne? Joanne?"

"Oh my God, is she dead?" Eddie asked.

"Oh my, this *is* dramatic," Number 5 said.

Then my mother said, "She's breathing. I think we need an ambulance."

Eddie looked around for the phone and found it sitting in its cradle on the desk. He dialed 911. I heard him giving the address to the dispatcher.

I hurried into the kitchen and poured a glass of water. It was kind of warm, so I opened the refrigerator and then the little freezer door within, plopping a couple of ice cubes into the glass. As I did, I noted that two casseroles were already in there, one with a portion taken out of it. They'd probably come from neighbors in the building.

Hurrying back in to the sofa, I put my hand over the glass and shook it a little to make the water colder.

Seeing what I was about to do, Number 5 said, "Oh, that's just cruel."

Then, keeping my hand over the glass, I dribbled the icy water onto Joanne's face. After a moment, she gasped, her eyes flying open.

"Joanne, Joanne, wake up."

"Arghllgar…" she said, or something similar.

"Joanne, did you take some pills?"

"Naw, ma gerr," she replied.

"Do you think you can sit up?" Then to my mother I said, "We should probably try to make her puke."

"Oh, dear."

"Or maybe walk her around." I was remembering a scene from *The Apartment*, one of our older videos that rented a lot. Perhaps not the best source of medical advice, but still—

I pulled on Joanne trying to get her up. I looked over at Number 5 and said, "Could you help?" Eddie was on the line with 911 telling them what we were doing.

"Fllmmmgglll…"

We got Joanne standing. Number 5 taking her under the left arm, while I took her under the right. After we went back and forth a few times, she suddenly vomited in the center of the living room.

"Okay, we have to put her down," I said, since we needed to clean her up. We put her into the black leather chair that was just like the one she'd sat in at Scottie's.

My mother had already run to the kitchen and was coming back with a roll of paper towels in one hand and a damp tea towel in the other. She handed me the paper towels while she used the damp towel to wipe Joanne's face and nightgown.

I heard a siren nearby, no more than a few blocks away. The ambulance would arrive soon. Eddie hung up the phone and said, "They're almost here. I'm going to open the lobby door for them." He slipped out of the apartment.

I laid a couple of sheets of paper towels over the vomit on

the floor. Holding my breath, I turned my head and scooped it up as best I could. I had a good view of the underside of the coffee table and space under the couch. It took a moment to register what I was looking at. And when it did register, it didn't really make sense. Right beneath the sofa were a couple of brown, fluted paper cups. The kind that came in candy boxes. Specifically, See's Candies. Jeffer used to buy me a box every so often. I knew they used the brown paper cups like that.

I rushed the puke-filled paper towels over to the garbage can in the kitchen and threw them in. Then I looked for a sponge. Finding one behind the faucet, I left the kitchen and was on my knees trying to clean the carpet, when two EMTs, both of whom looked as though they spent all of their off hours at the gym, hurried into the apartment.

"Do you know what she took?" the taller one asked.

"No, we just got here," my mother said.

I looked around for the box of candy. I didn't find it. While the EMTs worked on Joanne, occasionally asking questions, I stepped back into the kitchen and flipped open the garbage again. I got a nice whiff of bile from the vomit I'd just thrown in there. Holding my nose, I moved a few things around. I didn't see a box of See's Candies.

"What her name?"

"Joanne," my mother said.

I stayed in the kitchen. Casually, I opened the cupboards looking for the chocolates. Then I stopped. Feeling ridiculous. Those brown paper liners could have been there a long time. They could have come from a box that Rod ate months ago.

"Joanne, do you know where you are?"

"Rahhh," she said.

"This is her son's apartment. His name was Rod. He died three days ago," my mother explained.

"Are you saying Rod?" the shorter EMT asked.

"Rahhh."

"We're going to need to take her in." Then to his partner he added, "Let's get the gurney."

Before they could leave the apartment, Detective Amberson

walked in. The EMTs spent a moment explaining Joanne's condition to him and their plans to take her to the hospital. When he was done with the EMTs, Amberson turned to us and said, "Could you wait in the courtyard? This is a potential crime scene."

My mother, Number 5 and I filed out of the apartment. We sat down around one of the tables and watched as a few uniformed officers milled around. The landlord hadn't come back. I wondered if he'd gone back to hosing down the street.

"I'm confused," Number 5 said. "Why does he think that might be a crime scene? Does he think someone tried to kill her? Does he think someone killed Rod?"

"Do *you* think Rod was murdered?" I asked. This was certainly making my mind up.

He squinched his face—not a good look for him—and said, "You know, now that you mention it, I think a lot of people would have liked to kill Rod. Maybe someone did."

To my mother, I said, "I saw some of those little paper cups for candy on the floor. But I couldn't find a box anywhere."

"Is that important?"

"It might be."

"You think someone gave Joanne a box of poisoned candy?"

"Or drugged. And then they came back for it. When they were sure she was out of it. Yeah, I'm starting to think that. There were a couple of other casseroles in the fridge. People were bringing by food. Maybe someone brought candy, from See's. She wouldn't have thought it odd."

"What is See's?" my mother asked.

"Candy store."

"I love their peanut brittle," Number 5 said.

"How do you know it came from that store?"

"The paper cups were brown," I explained.

"But aren't they always brown?" Number 5 asked.

"No, they're always white."

"Oh no dear, that's not true."

I felt confused for a moment. I was sure I was right. And if I was wrong why did I think—

"The ones your father used to get me from Fannie Mae had the white cups. Maybe that's why you think they're always white. Except for the one's Jeffer bought you at—"

"See's."

"It's still a clue though," she went on. "Someone bought Joanne candy from somewhere and there's no box. And maybe there was something in the candy? But why though? Why would someone do that?"

"I don't know. But it does seem unlikely that a mother and son would overdose within days of each other. Doesn't it?"

Or maybe it wasn't that unlikely. Maybe it was even likely. I was feeling uncomfortably off-kilter, unsure if I knew the things I thought I knew. Trying to get back on track, I asked Number 5, "Did you notice anything last night?"

"I walked through around nine and saw there were lights on in Rod's apartment, and I know Greta brought her some dinner."

"Who is Greta?"

"Number 15. She's an old German woman. Numbers tattooed on her wrist. She swims every morning even when the pool is frigid."

"How do you know she brought Joanne dinner?"

"Well, I smelled it. It smelled delicious. She doesn't cook much for herself, so I was immediately suspicious. Then I heard her coming down the stairs. Oh, sorry, Number 5 is below Number 15. The whole building is that way."

"I see. What time was that?"

"Oh my, um, I'd guess six-ish."

"So, Joanne must have been back from Scottie's by six o'clock," I said to my mother.

Detective Amberson came out of Number 17 and down the stairs. His suit that day was beige, crisp and spotlessly clean. He looked like a catalog model. He glared at me and said, "You're Noah Valentine, aren't you?

"Yes, we've already met."

"Come over here, I'd like to talk to you privately."

I followed him over to the furthest corner of the pool. We

stood next to a concrete retaining wall. Above us was someone's backyard further up the hill.

"I got a call about you last night."

That got my attention. "Why would you get a call about me?"

"Detective Wellesley called saying she suspected you'd managed to access Rod Brusco's autopsy report. She wouldn't tell me how."

"I've never seen the report," I said truthfully. "Is there something important on it?"

He stared at me briefly, then continued, "Wellesley tells me you've stuck your nose into a couple of Rampart investigations. She doesn't like you much."

"No kidding."

"Well, that's her problem. I want to make something clear: This isn't Rampart. If you stick your nose into my investigation you're going to be sorry."

"Joanne is a friend of my mother's. That's really all that's going on," I said. It was sort of true. "And until a few minutes ago I was pretty sure that Rod's death was an accidental overdose."

"This doesn't mean it wasn't."

"I should tell you a couple of things. I overheard Tabitha and Allan next door talking. Someone was paying them to watch Rod or something; what it was wasn't clear. That someone is named Kiley or the Kileys. And this morning, while we were waiting for the ambulance, I noticed some brown paper cups under the sofa. The kind that come in a candy box. But I couldn't find a box of candy."

He scowled at me. "I just told you not to interfere."

"I'm not interfering. I'm telling you what I know." Well, not all of what I knew.

"Telling me about garbage you saw on the floor is interfering. Who knows how long that crap has been under the sofa? Could be a long time, don't you think?"

I'd considered that. And he was probably—

"No. No. They weren't there before. Scottie, Rod's ex-lover, said that Rod was on a detoxification diet. He wouldn't have been eating chocolate."

"You're saying you think there was something in the candy you can't find? Is that right?"

"At least talk to Tabitha and Allan."

"Oh I will. I'm going to talk to everyone. And you're going to keep your mouth shut."

And with that he walked away from me. I stood there a moment gathering my thoughts. I should probably call Javier and let him know what Detective Wellesley was up to. I wondered how much longer we needed to be there. At that moment, I wasn't sure if Amberson also wanted to talk to my mother. God, I hoped he didn't plan to threaten her too.

Amberson walked by the table where my mother still sat with Number 5 and up the steps to number 16. I walked around the pool and sat down again.

"I don't know what he thinks he's doing," Number 5 said. "They're not there."

"What do you mean they're not there?" I asked.

"They're in Palm Springs. Allan had a gig at The Barracks last night."

That kind of ruined my half-baked theory that they'd drugged a box of chocolates then given it to Joanne (as a peace-offering?) and then what? Climbed across their balcony to get the box of chocolates back once she'd passed out? Of course, if that didn't happen, what did?

"Wait. I thought you said he worked at the Hawk?"

"Oh he does. He'll be there tonight. Dancers like Allan flit all over the place. Palm Springs, San Diego, Long Beach. It keeps the customers from getting bored with the same old go-go boys every week."

Amberson stopped knocking on the door to Number 16 and came down the steps. He came over to our table giving me a dirty look. I nodded at Number 5, "He says they're in Palm Springs."

"Since yesterday," Number 5 supplied. I could tell he was lowering his voice and trying to sound butch.

Amberson hadn't stopped looking at me. The look made me hope I'd never be alone with him in a windowless interview room. Then, through gritted teeth, he said, "What's probably going on here is that Rod Brusco either accidentally or deliberately overdosed and his distraught mother has tried to kill herself a couple of days later."

"Oh no, that's not—" my mother started. Amberson shut her down with his death stare.

"Thanks for explaining that," I said. "Do you have everything you need from us? I'm wondering if we could go now?"

"Yeah, get out of here."

10

"WE SHOULD GO TO THE HOSPITAL. I HEARD THE attendant tell that detective they were going to Hollywood Community," my mother said as soon as we got into my car. "Do you know where that is?"

"It's in Hollywood somewhere," I guessed. "Does it matter, though? I don't think they'll let us see her. We're not family."

"We could lie," she suggested.

"Mother!"

"She shouldn't be alone, that's all."

We were silent for a moment, then she asked, "Are you going to do what that detective wants? Are you going to keep out of his investigation?"

"I guess so, sure." Probably not was a better answer, given my history.

"He's wrong, you know. Joanne did *not* try to kill herself. And that means Rod did *not* accidentally or deliberately overdose."

"I think you're right."

"And we're not going to do anything about it?"

I was driving south on Cahuenga, passing under the 101, and just after that there was a gas station. I pulled in. After I parked in front of a pump, I turned to my mother and said, "What do you think we should do about it?"

"I don't know. Can we call Detective Amberson's boss?"

"That's probably not a good idea. I doubt they'd do anything."

"So what can we do?"

"Well…nothing."

I opened my door to get out and my mother said, "If we're getting gas, let me pay for it."

"I wasn't—" I said, glancing at my gas gauge. "Oh, you know, I could use some gas."

My mother handed me a twenty.

"I don't need you to buy me gas."

"I know that. I want to. You're driving me all over the place, so I should contribute."

Actually, we'd been driving Joanne all over the place. Still, I gave up. It was easier to take the money—as Louis had learned the night before when he tried to pay for dinner. I hopped out of the car and went into the office portion of the station. The guy behind the cash register looked like he was also the main mechanic.

"Hi, I'd like ten dollars' worth on—" I looked over my shoulder. "Number 2."

He took the twenty from me.

"And do you know where Hollywood Community Hospital is?"

"Lungpay and Vine," he mumbled.

"Okay," I said, not sure that was helpful. He held out my ten dollars in change and I took it.

At the pump, I put ten dollars' worth into my tank. When I was done, I climbed into the car and held out the ten remaining dollars from the twenty my mother had given me.

"Oh you can keep that."

"I don't need an allowance, I'm not in high school."

"I know that. I just want to help."

I sighed heavily and crammed the money into a pocket. Making a left onto Cahuenga was not exactly fun, since I had to cross two lanes to get to the southbound side. I had a sudden thought. There was something I wanted to do. Something I didn't really want my mother tagging along for. Maybe this was an opportunity—

"Do you mind if I just drop you off at the hospital?"

"What are you going to do?"

"I should go to Pinx and give Mikey a lunch break." Not at all true. Mikey would have his lunch around two when Missy came on.

"All right. You can drop me off."

"Could you get the *Thomas Guide* out of the glove compartment?"

"The what?"

"It's a map. Except it's a book."

She looked at me skeptically and opened the glove compartment. She pulled out the spiral bound street atlas.

"Look up Lungpay."

"That's a street name?"

"That's what the guy said."

I crossed Franklin and at the next intersection turned east. Cutting over to Vine, I continued south, watching the street signs as I went.

"I'm not finding anything," my mother said.

"Well, go to the page for Vine. We're at Hollywood and Vine." And the traffic was thickening.

"Oh, I see how this works," she said, flipping through. "There's a page for each little part of L.A. How clever."

We were stopped at a red light, six cars back.

"You know, there's something I should have asked you before now," I said.

"What's that, dear?"

"You didn't give Joanne any more of your sleeping pills, did you?"

"Oh God, no. And I would have said. I mean, if this was all my fault, I would have said before now."

"Okay, I thought so, but it seemed a good idea to check."

The light turned and I continued south, Selma, Sunset.

"There's no Lungpay but there is a DeLongpre."

"That's it," I said, mere seconds before it appeared. "Left or right?"

"Oh, there's a red cross to the left."

I turned onto DeLongpre and found the hospital about halfway down the block. It was about six stories tall and looked more like an uninspired apartment building than a hospital.

My mother put the *Thomas Guide* back into the glove compartment and gathered up her purse. As she got out of the car, I said, "If you have any trouble call Marc and Louis. I'll know to check with them if something goes wrong."

She shook her head. "If I have any trouble, I'll call Pinx. That's where you're going to be anyway."

"Oh yeah, of course. I meant as a backup. In case I'm on my way back."

"How long do you think you'll be?" she asked.

"Two hours, maybe."

"All right dear. I'll see you then." She gave a little wave and shut the door. I sat there while she walked up to the entrance of the hospital and disappeared inside. I had the feeling she was going to get into Joanne's room. I just didn't know what lie she'd tell.

Making a U-turn, I went back out to Vine and took it south to Santa Monica Boulevard. Then I turned right, heading west.

Jeffer and I had owned a small Spanish-style house on Hayworth south of Willoughby. The house was West Hollywood-adjacent, though Jeffer always listed our address as West Hollywood as if annoying the postman would convince the powers-that-be to expand the city limits by a block.

When we started Pinx Video I spent a lot of time taking Santa Monica east to where it joined Sunset and then, a block later, turning onto Hyperion. Generally, it took twenty-five minutes, so it wasn't terrible. It did mean that I became very familiar with the sights of Santa Monica Boulevard, so I already knew West Hollywood Universal Church.

The building was notable not because it was particularly interesting in an architectural sense but because the former storefront shared a parking lot with The Pleasure Chest and was across the street from one of the very few remaining porn palaces, The Pussycat (aka TomKat), which showed gay pornos, very often the same ones I rented. The juxtaposition of the West Hollywood Universal Church with its poorly affixed crucifix on top and its risqué neighbors was what caught my attention whenever I drove by.

When I got there, I found a spot on the street right in front of The Pleasure Chest. After I locked my car and fed the meter —with some of the quarters my mother had brought—I walked back to the church. Other than the cross on top of the building, there wasn't much about the church that seemed religious.

I walked in and found that the frontmost part of the church was a sort of lobby. It was carpeted from wall to wall with a low-pile, industrial-grade carpet. At the front on either side of the door were two benches, presumably made from plywood and now covered in the same carpet. It was the same kind of look as the APLA waiting room where I'd gone to get my test results. I didn't like remembering that day and didn't like the lobby for reminding me.

In front of me was a set of double doors that were standing open, so I could see what was presumably the nave. It was a large, windowless room with dozens of metal folding chairs lined up in rows with an aisle between them. To my left at the farthermost edge of the building was an open hallway that led to the back of the building.

Looking down the hallway I saw four doors on the right, which clearly led to windowless offices. I started down the hallway and right away noticed that the first door stood open. Inside was a young woman, no more than twenty-four or twenty-five, behind a desk.

"Can I help you?"

"I'm looking for Best Lives. They meet here, don't they?"

"They do. But I'm not sure if anyone's here yet. Their first workshop is at noon." She glanced at her watch. "It's eleven-forty five. C.B. must be running late."

"C.B.?"

"He's the executive director. Well, he's everything from

janitor to executive director. His office is down the hall, the last door."

I thanked her and continued down the hall. C.B. Those were the initials on the card I'd taken out of Rod's jeans. So they knew each other. I was in the right place.

The rest of the doors were closed. The one at very end had a small sign on it that said BEST LIVES. I knocked but didn't get an answer. Not surprising; the girl in the front office had said she didn't think anyone was there. Yet. Someone, C.B., should arrive soon.

Next to the door was a bulletin board. I perused it. On a sheet of blue Xerox paper was a calendar printed out. I checked for today's events. In about a half an hour, a Men's Rap group was meeting, a group called Facilitating Your Medical Care started an hour and a half later, and then at three there was a group called Dating with HIV. There were flyers for A Course in Miracles Study Group that met on Tuesday nights, a memorial for someone named Fred Rosen, and an offer of discount vitamins. I heard some noise to my right and turned to see a tall man of around forty, who looked like he might have spent his formative years as a Broadway dancer, hurtling toward me. His arms were full of a briefcase and a stack of manila folders. His straight, blond, chin-length hair was flying everywhere.

"Hi! Are you waiting for me?"

"I think so."

"I'm Curtis Barry. People call me C.B." Juggling his things, he reached into a pocket and pulled out a set of keys. He opened the door.

"I'm Noah Valentine."

"Noah, it's nice to meet you." He plunked his things down on a very crowded desk. "If you wouldn't mind, I have to set up the chairs for the twelve o'clock Men's Rap. Is that what you're here for?"

He moved as he talked; in fact he never seemed to be still. I followed him until we were in the nave. "So we want to fold up most of the chairs and stack them on the sides of the room. When we're done, there should be about ten left in a circle."

"Okay," I said, folding a chair. "I'm not here for the Men's Rap though."

"Oh, okay," he said, quickly folding half a dozen chairs and stacking them. "Why are you here?"

"Do you know Rod Brusco?"

There was a moment of silence. If he denied knowing Rod I was ready to pull his card out of my pocket and yell "Liar!" Of course, I wasn't sure I was wearing the same jeans I'd been wearing—

"Why do you want to know that?"

"He died on Wednesday night."

This got him to stop what he was doing. "Oh, I see. I hadn't heard."

"So you did know him?"

"Yes, Rod has been coming in for a long time. Years. You're a friend of his?"

"A friend of the family."

"Normally, we're very protective of the people who come here. I'm sure you can see why?"

"Yes, I understand."

"It must've been sudden? The last time I saw him he looked good. Very good. I thought he was on the upswing—"

"He was murdered."

C.B. stopped what he was doing. He sat down in the chair he was about to fold. "Murdered? Really?"

"Yes, and his mother—who came in for Thanksgiving—it looks like someone may have tried to poison her."

"That's awful."

"Anything you can tell me about Rod, I'd appreciate."

"What kind of things do you want to know?"

"He's been coming in for years and he was HIV positive. How was his health? You said he looked good?"

"Yes, but that doesn't always mean what we think. When he started coming his health wasn't good. AZT had stabilized him, but it was taking its toll. I think his doctor had talked him into a very high dosage. About a year ago, maybe less, he stopped going to the doctor and focused on vitamins, healthy living, A Course in Miracles, things like that."

"And that worked?"

"I don't know. He looked healthier, happier. It could have been a placebo effect. It never lasts."

"Do you know of anyone who might have wanted to hurt him? Someone who was jealous of him? Angry at him?"

"He was charismatic. Guys liked him; sometimes a little too much. There were a few small squabbles. A couple of guys stopped coming to Men's Rap because of him."

"It seems like he had a lot of money for a while, but he lost it. Do you know anything about that?"

"That kind of thing happens a lot."

"What do you mean?"

"I don't know for sure that Rod did this, but a lot of guys who have term life insurance will sell the policies for a portion of their face value. If you have a two hundred thousand dollar policy, an investor will give you a hundred and twenty-five. You make them the beneficiary. When you die they make a profit."

"What happens if you don't die?" I asked.

"Your investors have to be patient."

That seemed like a really good reason to kill someone to me. Was that who the Kileys were? Investors? Then something occurred to me. Joanne had made a big deal about being the beneficiary. So Rod couldn't have sold his insurance, right?

"You know there was this guy who came to a few meetings, I think it was in 1990. Shady character. He talked about being a kind of matchmaker for guys with AIDS and investors."

"What was his name?"

"I don't remember. I threw him out after he came a few times. Told him not to come back. A friend of mine is an insurance agent and he said the legit way these worked was to carve them up so one guy had thirty investors rather than one. It spreads the risk out that way."

"But that's not the way this guy worked."

"I don't think so. I mean, he never made his pitch to me personally, but I heard things."

"Would Rod have been able to change the beneficiary? You know, after taking the money?"

"I don't think so. It would kind of defeat the point. But again, this was so shady. It's hard to say."

"Do you have any idea how I could find this guy?"

"I don't." He stood up and looked over my shoulder. "Welcome. It's Tim, isn't it?" I turned and there was an average looking guy lingering at the door, the kind of guy who always played the next-door neighbor on sitcoms. "Come on in."

Then to me he said, "You're welcome to stay for the rap."

"Oh, no, I don't think so."

"Ah, so you're *not*—"

He was politely asking if I was HIV positive. Honestly, I was tempted to lie. I don't know why, there was no reason to.

"Um. I am. I just don't need to talk about it."

"Ah. Well, if you ever do. Come back. We'd be glad to see you." Then he smiled, a broad, happy thing. "I mean, I'd be glad to see you."

11

DRIVING AWAY, I TRIED NOT TO THINK ABOUT THE attractive man who'd clearly been flirting with me. Instead, I went over everything I'd learned. I had to find out more about term life insurance. Most importantly, I had to find a way to learn who Rod's investor was. I remembered seeing a folder in the back of his car, but I couldn't remember the name of the investment firm. What was it? Did it start with a C? Carmichael? Carlyle? Carson? None of those were right. So what was right?

At Vine I turned north, but instead of turning onto DeLongpre and heading to the hospital, I cut over to Cahuenga and drove north to The Pagoda. As I approached, I saw that there were still two black-and-whites sitting on one side of the building so there didn't seem much point in stopping. I made a very illegal U-turn and pulled up right behind Rod's BMW.

I hurried in front of my car and walked into the carport. I didn't have to get too close to the BMW to see the broken glass on the ground and that the back passenger window was gone. I looked into the car. The investment folder was gone too.

I went back to my car and sat for a bit. I had the eerie, uncomfortable feeling that someone was one step ahead of me. A someone who had probably killed Rod and attempted to kill Joanne. A someone who was cleaning up any evidence that might lead to their getting caught. A someone who knew what I was thinking. Except, of course, they couldn't. I hadn't planned on going to Best Lives until I left the house and I'd told no one. And, no one knew what C.B. said to me. Nor did they know I was going to stop at Rod's apartment to get the name of the investment firm—I didn't know until I turned north on Vine. So maybe it wasn't that someone was always one step ahead of me. It might just be that I was always one step behind.

When I got to the hospital, I parked in the lot next to it. Walking into the emergency room, I remembered I didn't know Joanne's real last name. Or I remembered that I'd forgotten it. I was pretty sure she'd said it at some point, but everyone kept calling her Mrs. Brusco so that's the name that stuck in my head. But that wasn't her name. I tried to remember what her name really was. Jackson? Grant? I avoided the receptionist's desk and walked through the waiting room looking for my mother. She wasn't there. That meant she was either in the ER with Joanne or they'd admitted Joanne and they were both upstairs somewhere.

I bit the bullet and went over to the receptionist. "A woman of about seventy named Joanne came in about an hour ago, maybe an hour and a half. There was a slightly younger woman with her."

"What's the woman's last name?"

"I don't know it. I'm just a family friend."

"And you don't know the family name?"

"She's been married several times and I don't know which name is her legal name right now."

"Okay. What name do you have?"

"Brusco, Joanne Brusco." I knew that wasn't going to work but it's all I had.

The woman looked at the screen in front of her. After a moment, she said, "I have a Joanne Lincoln."

"Yes, that's her. She's still down here?"

"Yes."

"Can I go back?"

"We only let family accompany a patient into the ER."

"My mother's with her though."

"Your mother? I remember her. She told me she was Mrs. Lincoln's sister."

"Oh, yes, she is. She's Joanne's sister."

"Your Aunt Joanne? Whose last name you don't know?"

I stood there for a second wondering how to get out of this. "Our family is complicated. You see, my mother and my aunt are actually half-sisters, different fathers, different last names. And then my aunt has been married three times and my mother twice. Honestly, half the time these women don't know their *own* names."

She gave me a sour look. I doubted she believed a word of the ridiculous lie I'd just told her, but I had given her enough information to keep her out of trouble if I became a nuisance.

"Mrs. Lincoln is in bed three. Through the double doors."

"Thank you."

I walked around the reception desk and through the double doors. There were beds behind drapes on each side of me. I didn't see any numbers. I counted down three beds and looked at the bed on my left: The drape was pulled and I didn't see any sign of life. I looked to my right: The drape was also pulled, but I recognized my mother's feet. She'd left the house in a pair of leather sandals, beige culottes and a peach shell—those were definitely her sandals. I slipped around the drape and saw I was right. My mother was standing next to Joanne's bed.

"Oh, hello dear. You're back early."

"It didn't take as long as I thought."

"Traffic was light?"

"Very," I said, remembering that I'd told her I was going to Silver Lake to give Mikey a lunch break, which would not have been possible in the scant hour I'd been gone. "Actually, I forgot that there were two people working today, so they can give each other breaks. I drove part way there and then I turned around."

She just smiled at me. I began to wonder if I was a bad liar. I mean, I could tell she knew I was lying and the receptionist had certainly known. Did I need to hone my lying skills?

"How is Joanne?" I asked, changing the subject.

"I'm fine," Joanne said.

"Oh my God, you *are* better."

"I want to go home."

"Joanne, what happened last night after we left?" I asked.

"Oh, I had…fun. Rod's… what's the word? People who live near."

"Neighbors," my mother suggested.

"Yes, Rod's neighbors are so nice! We sat outside and conversed, conversated—"

"Talked."

"Yes, we talked."

"You don't mean his next-door neighbors, do you?"

"No, no they're…bad. I mean Eddie and his wife Consuelo —they speak English so well."

I resisted the temptation to point out that Mexican-Americans in California had often been there for three or four generations and sometimes didn't even speak Spanish anymore.

"Greta made a casserole for me. What a life she's had. And then there was Paul, Peter—Palmer maybe? Anyway, he was a very nice boy."

"Which one of them gave you the chocolates?"

"None of them."

"Then who did?"

"I don't know. They were just there, on the doorstep. It was very late. Someone knocked; I wasn't even sure at first I'd heard it, and when I got to the door they were gone and there were the chocolates. Wait? Do you think they were—?"

"Yes. I do."

"Someone drugged me?"

"I think so." Then I asked, "So, did you tell anyone else about being the beneficiary on Rod's insurance?"

"Why shouldn't I tell people? I want them to know that Rod was a good boy who took care of his mother."

"Of course you do," I said. I wanted to be careful how much I said. Even though I hadn't known Rod, I wanted to keep his secret.

A young doctor in scrubs eased through the drape. He had a clipboard in hand and was reading it.

Joanne didn't wait for him to finish reading. "When I can I leave?"

"Well, let's see. Probably not before Tuesday."

"Tuesday! No, I want to go home now."

"We don't recommend that."

"I don't care what you recommend. I want to leave."

"I'm afraid you can't. The LAPD has placed you under a 5150 hold due to a suspected suicide attempt."

"That's ridiculous! I didn't try to kill myself. I just ate some chocolates. Someone *else* was trying to kill me."

"That's not what the detective is telling us."

"Joanne, maybe it's better that you're here," I suggested. "Nobody can kill you if you're in here."

"Except the doctors."

The doctor took that as a cue to leave, saying, "An orderly will be in soon to take you to our psychiatric department."

Then he walked out of the room.

"They're putting me in the nuthouse."

"I'm sure it's nothing like that," my mother said. "You'll just spend a couple of days resting, which might be a very good thing."

"You know I feel like I've gotten a lot of rest in the last few days. That nap I took after the Valium and then last night."

She was probably right about that. My mother looked quite contrite. She said, "We'll go back to the apartment and get your luggage for you."

I envisioned having to schlep around Joanne's luggage yet again.

"It may still be a crime scene," I said.

"Oh that's true. Joanne, we'll get your things as soon as we can."

"Thank you."

I WAS ABOUT to start the car when my mother asked, "So where did you go, really?"

"It's not important."

"Why did you ask if she'd told anyone about the insurance? Why is that important?"

I sighed heavily. "Remember I told you Rod was HIV positive. It was about that."

"Oh, I see."

I started the car, giving her a bit of time to absorb that information. When we got to Vine, I began to explain, "I went to this group that Rod was involved with, Best Lives. It's for people with HIV. The guy who runs the place told me that some guys who have AIDS have been selling their life insurance so that they have money to live out their lives. The investor pays a portion of the face value and they become the beneficiary. When the guy dies they make a profit."

"That's horrible. How can people stand to profit from AIDS?"

I shrugged, not mentioning that hospitals, doctors and drug companies were all profiting and not always helping much; if at all.

"So, whoever bought Rod's insurance may have gotten tired of waiting for him to die. And then Joanne was boasting about Rod's insurance money like it was hers. Does that mean it was someone at the table last night?"

"Not necessarily. It was a warm night, people's windows were open, a lot of people could have heard what Joanne was saying."

"Her voice does carry. Now, if Rod made her the beneficiary after he sold his policy would that be legal?"

"Probably not. I'd guess there's language in whatever he signed that says he can't do that."

"But he did it anyway."

I shrugged. "Maybe he was hoping to gum up the works or maybe he actually thought he could change it. Just because he signed something doesn't mean he understood it."

"Do you think Joanne will be safe in the hospital?" my mother asked.

"Well, I think she's going to be careful about what she eats."

"That's not the only way to kill someone."

"No. But whoever killed Rod, whoever tried to kill Joanne, they want to get away with it. They're not going to walk into the psych ward with a gun. They're not going to try and stab her. They'd want to do something they can get away with."

"Since it's a psych ward, do you think they lock the patients in their rooms?"

"Maybe. I don't know."

"She might be safer that way."

"When we get home you can call and find out about visiting."

DEAN MARTIN WAS SINGING "LET It Snow! Let It Snow! Let It Snow!" when we reached the top of the red stairs. Marc was flocking the windows of their apartment. Since we'd left, an aluminum Christmas tree had appeared and been decorated in red ornaments; a toy train set was running in and out of the birds of paradise and banana trees.

"There you are!" Marc called to us. "Sit down, Louis is bringing out some lunch. Just leftovers from Thursday, nothing fancy."

I looked at my mother, who said, "We do need to catch them up."

"Oh, that's right." I turned back to Marc, "Joanne is in the hospital."

"Oh my God! What happened?" He stopped flocking.

"She's going to be okay. We think someone put something into a box of chocolates and left it at her door."

"You mean they tried to poison her?"

"Drug is more accurate."

"Another overdose?"

We sat down at the table and caught Marc up on our morning. "Obviously it's the same person who killed Rod," he said. "Do you think Joanne knows more than she's said?"

"I'm not sure," I said. "She might know something and not know she knows. Does that make sense?"

"Unfortunately, it does," he replied. "Poison is a woman's crime, you know."

"Is that from *Quincy*?" I asked.

"I don't know. It might have been Sherlock Holmes."

"I've heard that too," my mother said.

"But Rod may have been killed with a pillow," I suggested. "Could a woman have done that?"

"If he was drunk enough," Marc said.

"Men always underestimate women."

"Mom, everyone knows women don't have a lot of upper body strength."

"Well who's to say the killer didn't put the pillow on his face and then sit on it?"

That was an interesting theory.

"One thing," my mother said. "Whoever it is, he or she doesn't want to face their victims. Does that mean anything?"

Louis came out of their apartment and set a platter down in the center of the table. On it was a bright yellow jumble on top of a pile of rice.

"Oh my, doesn't that look exotic."

"Louis, this isn't leftovers," I said.

"It's turkey curry," Louis explained. "The turkey, the peas, the mushrooms, all leftovers. Everything else I just happened to have in the cupboard."

Marc gave us a look and said, "Yes, my lover is the kind of man who just happens to have coconut milk in the cupboard."

"They sell it at Trader Joe's," Louis explained.

"That doesn't mean anyone knows what to do with it. I'll bet half the people in Silver Lake bought a can and poured it on their Special K."

"So this is Indian food?" my mother asked.

"Well, I wouldn't call it authentic. But it's in that spirit," Louis explained.

"Enough about the food," Marc said. Then to Louis, "You didn't hear; Joanne is in the hospital."

Then we caught Louis up on what had happened to Joanne and how she was doing, along with our various theories about the killer. As we did, we dished out lunch and took a few exploratory bites.

"Oh, this is very interesting," my mother said, meaning the food. I'd had curry before and liked it. I wasn't as sure it liked me.

"Tell them about the insurance," my mother prompted.

"Well, Rod's ex told me that Rod was HIV positive and... that he'd sold his life insurance policy."

"How does that work?" Marc asked.

"I don't know much about it, but I think there are companies that connect dying people to an investor."

"So then he wasn't just HIV positive. He had AIDS," Louis pointed out.

"Yes," I said. That embarrassed me. I should be making that distinction. Especially in front of my mother. Being HIV positive didn't mean you had AIDS. At least, not yet.

"There was a folder in the back of Rod's car from an investment firm, but someone smashed his window and took it."

"How do you know that?" my mother asked.

"I stopped on the way back to the hospital."

"Do you remember the name of the firm?" Louis asked.

"I don't. I remember the folder was blue, the lettering gold, but for the life of me I can't think of the name."

"Was it one word or two?"

"It was Something Investments."

"A long word or a short word."

"Medium."

"Do you think it started with a vowel or a consonant?"

"Louis, I don't remember." I really was trying.

"Who wants wine?" Marc asked.

"It's barely noon," my mother said.

"And you're on vacation."

Marc got up and ran inside for wine and glasses.

"This curry dish is so good."

"Thank you, Angie." Then Louis turned to me and said, "Grr-Grr-Grr-Ba-Ba-Ba."

"Stop it. I'll remember eventually."

"What if we get the phonebook and read every investment firm listed?"

I raised my eyebrows at him. "You have no other plans for the day?"

Marc was back with wine and glasses. He handed out the glasses saying, "This is a pinot grigio, very light. You'll hardly know you're drinking."

"You know, it really doesn't matter if I can remember the name of the investment firm or not. Rod's death is suspicious. The insurance company probably won't pay until they're sure it was a natural death." I took a sip of the wine. I recognized it as the one they always got from Trader Joe's.

"Not necessarily," Louis said. "Whoever killed Rod knows more than we do. Or at least they think they do. The coroner could still decide Rod's death was an accidental overdose. You can lace marijuana with heroin. And we know that Rod was still smoking dope, so it's possible there will be heroin in his system, and marijuana and alcohol. It could end up being called an accidental overdose even if it is really murder."

"You mean, someone could have slipped him some heroin-laced marijuana," I said.

"Exactly."

"And it could all take months to sort out. In the meantime, someone's trying to kill Joanne," Marc said.

"You should tell the police what you know," Louis said.

"I tried. Detective Amberson isn't very receptive. He told me I'd be sorry if I stuck my nose into his case."

"Is that what he was saying to you?" my mother asked. "And he looked like such a nice man."

"Well, you can tell Javier," Louis said.

"No, I can't. I think I got him trouble. Detective Wellesley found out about the autopsy and she called Amberson."

"You should still tell him."

Something about the way he said that made me ask, "Why do you—what's going on?"

"We're all going to New York, New York later."

"They're having a champagne bust. As much as you can drink for ten dollars," Marc added.

I cringed. "That sounds horrible. Cheap champagne doesn't get better just because there's more of it." Of course, that wasn't the reason I didn't want to go.

"Javier's going to be there," Louis said.

And that was the reason I didn't want to go.

"It does sound fun," my mother said.

"I don't know."

"Oh come on," Louis said. "Your mother wants to come. It'll be a blast."

And since my mother hadn't exactly had a blast on this trip, I agreed that we'd go.

12

THANKFULLY, NEW YORK, NEW YORK HAD NOT YET decorated for Christmas. There was still a cardboard turkey over the bar, and yellow and orange streamers. The place was packed, of course, and Whitney Houston wailed about how she'd always love us. The bar had bought plastic champagne "glasses" for the bust and a tall, pretty cocktail waiter squeezed his way through the crowd filling glasses.

My mother, who had dressed very carefully, looked smart in a black-and-white houndstooth, two-piece suit. Before we left the apartment she'd asked me, "Will there be lesbians there?"

"Not a lot, Mom."

"That's good."

"You don't like lesbians?"

"Oh, no dear, they're fine. It's this suit. It's a little mannish and I don't want to send out the wrong signals."

"Uh-huh." I decided not to explain that not all lesbians were 'mannish' or interested in mannish women, and that it would probably take more than a tailored suit to allow her to pass as a lesbian. As it turned out there were only four women in the bar, and my mother and Tina were two of them. We'd just finished explaining to Tina and Leon about the insurance and the payout and all that.

"You're talking about viatical settlements," Leon said.

"How do you know about those?" Louis wanted to know.

"I have other friends, you know. I don't simply disappear the moment I walk out of your courtyard."

"All right, what else do you know?"

"They were more popular before AZT. Investors like to be sure you're going to drop dead. I mean, AZT isn't saving anyone fast, but it does seem to slow things down. So if you're hoping to make a quick forty or fifty thousand in a few months it's a bummer."

"What about the Kileys?" my mother asked. "Could they be the investors?"

"Who are the Kileys?" Tina asked.

"We don't really know," my mother said. "But they paid Rod's neighbors in number 16 enough to go on an expensive vacation."

"Except it doesn't make sense anymore. Whoever killed Rod also drugged Joanne, and it wasn't the neighbors because they were in Palm Springs last night. They weren't there to hear Joanne talk about the insurance and they weren't there to drug her."

"Of course, Palm Springs is only two hours away," Leon said. "You drive over, check into your hotel. Come back and leave the drugs for Joanne, wait a bit, collect them, and then head back to Palm Springs. You could even tell the desk clerk what a wonderful hike you took on the Tahquitz trail."

"Have you done this before?" Louis asked. "You certainly seem to know what you're talking about."

"'I was in Palm Springs' is my alibi for everything."

"There's another option," Marc said. "Allan could have stayed in Palm Springs to do his gig, establishing their alibi. Tabitha could have driven back to L.A. No one at the hotel would notice that she was gone for five hours. It wouldn't seem strange."

"Why wouldn't she stay to watch her husband dance?" my mother asked.

"Oh, no, no, no," Leon said. "The Barracks is not the kind of place where you bring your wife."

"Oh, I see," she said. I really hoped she didn't.

"Then why did she go at all?" Tina asked.

We all shrugged—and then my heart did a jumping jack in my chest. Two men were walking toward us. One was Javier in a tight black T-shirt and a pair of 501s. The other was a wall of muscle with strawberry blond hair clipped close to his head. The Wall wore a tank top even though it was November and not especially appropriate for New York, New York, though I doubted anyone was going to correct him. *This must be the boyfriend* was my first thought. Then I wondered what Javier had ever seen in me. The Wall and I could have been entirely different species. It didn't make sense that someone who liked me could also be attracted to this man.

Javier smiled at us and said, "This is my friend Tim."

Everyone said 'hello' and gave their name. What was he doing? I wondered. And then I thought, he's moving through things very quickly. Too quickly. When I met him in the spring he barely knew how to stand in a gay bar. Then I saw him again in the summer and he was putting himself on display at Gay Pride wearing tiny shorts and no shirt. And now he showed up with this 'boyfriend,' who looked like something out of a muscle magazine. It was like Javier had gone from Gay 101 to graduate study in less than six months.

I could feel his eyes on me, so I smiled and said, "So, what do you do, Tim?"

"I'm a court reporter."

"Oh, well that must be interesting."

"Not usually. Real trials are very dull."

I'd always thought of court reporters as people who should be invisible and go unnoticed. How could anyone see the judge past this giant of a guy? Not to mention, didn't court reporters work on tiny little typing machines? Even this guy's fingers were huge.

"Is that how you met?" Leon asked Javier. "Was he deposing you?"

"The lawyers are the ones who depose. I just write it all down."

"We met at the Faultline," Javier said.

"How romantic," Leon said. Though I'd never thought of meeting in a leather bar as romantic. Through a tight smile, Leon continued, "Personally, I prefer the Gauntlet for romance."

Then he launched into a monologue on the various merits and demerits of the Faultline vs. the Gauntlet. It gave Javier an opportunity to move toward me and then pull me away, saying, "You're causing a stir at Hollywood Division."

"I'm sorry I got you in trouble."

"No, I'm sorry. Wellesley found the autopsy report in the fax machine. She backed me into a corner and I had to tell her the truth. I didn't think she'd go after you like that."

"I appreciate what you did. I won't ask you for anything else."

"That isn't why I brought it up. I'm worried about you. Amberson isn't someone you mess with."

"I know. He's already threatened me."

"Take that seriously. He won't hesitate to arrest you."

"Arrest me? For what?"

"Witness tampering for one."

"We're not telling people what to say. We're just asking questions."

"He doesn't have to get a conviction to cause you trouble. Do you want to spend a night in jail? Do you want to post bail? Do you want to hire an attorney?"

"No. I don't want to do any of those things."

"Then you'd be smart to keep out of this."

"But I don't think he's really doing anything. He put a 5150 on Joanne even though she didn't try to kill herself."

"I don't know that Amberson agrees with you. And her son did just die. People who try to commit suicide don't always tell the truth."

Then I explained to him all about the insurance and about Joanne thinking she was the beneficiary even though she might not be anymore. The waiter came by and refilled my glass—Javier and his boyfriend were drinking long-necked beers. I glanced over and saw that Tim and Louis were having an intense conversation, while my mother and Tina were whispering to each other—or rather yelling in each other's ears. The last thing I remember Javier saying to me before the crowd shifted and we were all talking to other people was, "We have to be careful. There are things going on at Rampart. Bad things."

Then he was gone and I found myself standing with Marc, so I asked, "What are Louis and Tim talking about?"

"Sinead O'Connor," he said, rolling his eyes. I remembered that she'd done something outrageous on *Saturday Night Live* the month before. The staff at Pinx talked about it for days. And even so, I couldn't remember exactly what she'd done.

"Is Louis for or against?"

"For. Or rather, for freedom of speech."

"And Tim is Catholic?"

"I don't know. I heard him say something about politeness." He shrugged. "Maybe he just doesn't like women who shave their heads."

The boy with the champagne came our way again and refilled our drinks. They didn't give us very big glasses, but they came by a lot. I tried to figure out how many glasses I'd had, but then my mother was standing next to me saying, "So that's your policeman. I see why you like him."

"I don't—there's nothing going on. That's his boyfriend he's with."

"Oh, that's not going to last."

"Mom, what do you know about it?"

"I wasn't born yesterday. See, in every couple there's a pretty one. Tim thinks he's the pretty one but he's not. As soon as he figures that out, it's over."

"Really?"

"Mark my words. I was the pretty one in my marriage and we both knew it. Your father didn't mind at all."

"What about me and Jeffer?"

"Jeffer was the pretty one, dear. But you knew that, didn't you?"

I supposed I did, though I had the feeling she wasn't only talking about looks. Jeffer was good-looking, but he also got all the attention no matter what. And my mother certainly got more attention than my father. Which I guess meant I was like my father. Did I want to be like him? He'd always seemed kind of dull, to be honest. But maybe it was better to be dull than—

Leon bought us a round of shots. I don't know what they were, but they were sickly sweet. Tina came over to say good-bye.

"I'm swamped with work. I have to go home and read something called *Dwayne's Planet*. The hottest script in town is a satire of a satire." She shook her head in disbelief. "So nice to see you again, Angie." She air-kissed my mother. Then to me she said, "Call me and tell everything about this murder you guys are talking about. It sounds so much better than anything I'm reading."

And then just a little while later, or maybe it was an hour—I was losing track of time—we were climbing into two cars, all of us, Javier and Tim included. I wasn't entirely sure where we were going. I guess I'd had a lot of champagne. And shots. There'd been another round of—

"Where are we going?" I asked at least three times. I was in Marc's backseat wedged between my mother and Leon, when I was finally told, "The Hawk."

"Oh no, no, we should *not* go there."

For a myriad of reasons.

THE HAWK WAS LOCATED on the very edge of West Hollywood. It had probably once been what was called a fern bar, a woodsy, open kind of place with lots of hanging plants. Somewhere along the line the flora died, the windows got tinted nearly black, and a layer of grit was allowed to settle over the place. In the back of *Frontiers Magazine*, The Hawk was described as a Levi/leather bar with cheap beer and a bad reputation.

At the door, we were stopped by a three hundred and fifty

pound bouncer who'd spread himself over a stool. He looked our group over and zeroed in on my mother.

"Can I see two forms of identification? With pictures," he said to her. No one had that. It was just a way to keep women out of the bar.

"Seriously?" Louis said. "She's my mother. She's old enough to drink."

I was kind of drunk, but I was pretty sure she was *my* mother so I said so, "Wait, she's my mother."

"No, she's my mother," Marc said.

"You're all wrong. She's *my* mother," Leon said.

Our mother began to giggle.

"Jesus Christ," the bouncer said.

When our little *Spartacus* moment was over, my mother said, "It's all right boys. I have two picture IDs." Then she opened her purse and dug out her wallet.

"You do?" I said. "Nobody has two picture IDs."

"Actually, I have three. I have my Michigan state license and one for the senior center, and then one for the junior college. I took a film appreciation class there—it was very disappointing. The instructor only seemed to appreciate movies that didn't make sense."

The bouncer frowned and took my mother's IDs. He was still looking for a reason not to let her in. That was annoying me. I thought bringing my mother inside was a horrible idea, but I was the one who should be stopping her, not him.

Glancing up at us he said, "Look, I don't care whose mother she is, but I gotta ask, do you really want to bring your mother in there?"

"We just want to see one of the dancers."

"You wanna see one— this ain't Chippendales, you know"

"Young man, I've been looking at naked men since before you were born," my mother said.

He closed his eyes and shook his head. "Please don't stay long. I need this job."

"Thank you."

We walked into the bar. It was a large room with a couple of

French doors on the far side opening into a courtyard. The place had been painted flat black, had camouflage netting on the walls, and a small square bar in the center of the room. Louis asked what we wanted from the bar—I asked for a Calistoga, my mother asked for a vodka on the rocks when Louis told her they probably didn't have a nice dry white. He and Marc went over to the bar.

"I don't know why that young man made a fuss," my mother said. "I'm sure there's nothing in here I haven't—oh, dear."

I followed her look across the room to a young man who was attached to the wall about two feet off the floor. He had at least three dozen clothespins attached to his nearly naked body. Each pin pinching about two inches of skin. On his face was an expression somewhere between pain and pleasure.

Since I had no idea what to say to my mother about that, I said, "We should collect our thoughts. We need to think about what we want to ask Allan." I didn't add, mainly so we could get out of there quickly.

"We should probably ask if he has any dance training," she suggested.

"Really?"

"As a warm up. You never start with the tough questions. You have to gain their trust."

"Really?"

"You know I just adore *Matlock*," she explained.

I shook my head—but quickly decided that was a bad idea. All the champagne I'd had was making me queasy. Or maybe it was the shots. Did I have a vodka drink too?

That reminded me—where had Leon gone to? I looked around and saw that he was near the entrance talking to Javier and Tim, who must have come in right after us. I wanted to go home. I wondered how long it would take for a cab to show up if I called one right then.

"We need him to tell us everyone who was at the party Wednesday night," my mother said. "And who the Kileys are."

Just then the techno music that had been playing stopped

and an announcer introduced the next dancer over the P.A. system. The first part of what he said was too garbled to understand, so I didn't hear much more than, "Give it up for Zeus!"

My first thought was that Allan wouldn't be coming on until later, but then out he came in a military-themed outfit and climbed onto a podium across the room from the guy attached to the wall. I wondered if Mr. Clothespins was annoyed by the dancers since they tended to pull the focus off him. I mean, if you allow yourself to be stuck on a wall in a busy bar and pinched by dozens of clothespins, it has to be a little about the attention. Right?

I watched Allan begin to writhe to the unfamiliar music. Some kind of heavy duty dance mix that was lost on me. The thing that wasn't lost on me was the name Zeus. Zeus! Why would he call himself that? I mean, yes, I could see why he might want a pseudonym, but why a Greek god? I mean, that was kind of a lot to live up to.

Rather quickly he unbuttoned his shirt and slipped out of it. That left an army cap, pants and boots. That wasn't really a lot to take off and I began to worry about how he'd be getting out of the boots. Would he sit down on the edge of the podium to untie them? Slowly, he unzipped his pants and I could see a pair of camo briefs underneath. The answer to how he'd be dealing with his boots came a few moments later when he yanked his pants off in one move. Velcro, apparently.

"It's nice to see he has a gimmick, but he should probably have called himself Sergeant Zeus," Marc said, as he and Louis returned from the bar with the cocktails. I was handed my soda water.

Sipping my chilled water, I felt incredibly self-conscious watching a male stripper with my mother seated right next to me. I tried not to watch her watch him. We were standing behind a number of men, so I didn't think Allan had seen us. Louis leaned over holding out a five dollar bill.

"Do you want to let him know we're here?"

"I don't know," I admitted. Then I leaned over and told my mother, "You're supposed to tip them."

"I know. I watch Sally Jessy Raphael."

I turned back to Louis and said, "Should we try to find him later in his dressing room?"

"I don't know that they actually have a dressing room here."

I looked around. That made sense. Zeus might have changed in the men's room. Or maybe they had a little manager's office like I had at Pinx. Or maybe he just showed up like that.

The briefs came off—well, he ripped them off, leaving him in just his boots and a tiny little black thong. His ass was nicely tanned, so I had to assume he'd spent time tanning on his deck at The Pagoda. He was also beginning to sweat. A line began to form, so I decided I'd better go up and see if we could talk to him afterward. I grabbed the five from Louis and slipped through the crowd until I was standing behind two guys, one of whom slipped a couple dollars into Allan's thong and then ran a finger all around it. When he'd had enough, Allan leaned over and gave the man a kiss on his bald head.

Then it was my turn. I stepped forward with the five dollar bill folded between my fingers. At first he saw only the cash. Taking my hand, he guided it toward the pouch of his thong. Before I knew it I found myself groping him, as he expertly used his fingers to push the five dollar bill into the pouch. I was thoroughly humiliated and sure that Louis had given me a five for just that reason—the other guy, with his lone single, had gotten a chaste kiss on the head.

I looked up into Allan's face and he recognized me.

"When you're done, we need to ask you some questions."

I expected that would get him to let go of my hand so I could stop feeling him up. And it did. But I did not expect him to jump off the podium and run through the crowd and out the front door. Javier was right behind him. I ran after the two of them.

Outside it was dark and chilly, the temperature having dropped quickly when the sun went down. I was sorry I hadn't worn a jacket—although I probably wasn't as sorry as Allan bolting down Santa Monica Boulevard in nothing but army boots and a thong. Javier was a few feet behind him, while I was at least twenty feet further behind. I glanced over my shoulder and noticed that none of my friends were following. Apparently no one else wanted to be separated from their drinks.

Allan dashed around a corner and Javier followed closely behind. By the time I caught up to them, Javier had Allan shoved up against the hood of a sleek, black sports car. Somewhere along the way, Allan's thong had broken and he was using both hands to cover his junk.

"Why are you running?!" Javier yelled. "Tell me! Why?!"

From the hood of the car, Allan took one hand off his junk, raised a finger and pointed it at me. "Him."

"Him? What about him?"

"He told people I killed Rod Brusco. He told the cops."

"Did you kill him?"

"NO!"

"Who are the Kileys then?" I asked.

"That's none of your business."

"Did they pay you to kill Rod?"

"What? No. That's crazy." He sighed. "The Kileys are this nice couple from Encino. They lived in Rod's apartment when they were first married. Their daughter wants to move to Hollywood and be an actress. They want to rent Rod's apartment. They're sentimental."

"And they're paying you enough to go to Belize?"

"A thousand bucks. It's the off-season. The tickets are a hundred and fifty each. The hotel is practically free."

"Why wouldn't they just go to Eddie and ask him to call them?"

"Oh, well, we sort of told them we were the managers. Can you let me up now?"

Javier reluctantly let go of him. Allan stood up, struggling to keep himself covered as he did. To Javier he said, "Who are you anyway?"

"I'm a police officer and I could arrest you for indecent exposure right now."

"So this was some kind of undercover sting?"

"Except I'm not arresting you. Who else was at your party the night Rod died?"

"I don't know, it was packed. We have a lot of friends. We're popular. I mean, what do you want, a list?"

"Yes, we do," Javier said.

"Oh, come on. Most of the people there were just friends of me and Tabitha. They didn't even know Rod before the party."

"All right, so aside from those friends. What about people who did know Rod?"

"There were a lot of people from the building,"

"Anyone acting suspicious?" Javier asked. It was a very cop-like question.

"Just Rod. I mean, he wasn't really drinking anything, just talking about this new diet he was on and how it was making him feel great. I mean, like all of a sudden he's this health nut."

"Can you make us a list of the people who were there?"

"I left my pen in my other pants," he said, dryly.

"Later. Can you make us a list later?"

"Yeah, sure, whatever. My last show is at one, I can do it after that."

"How about I swing by your apartment in the morning?"

"Oh man, my wife will be there."

"Maybe I'd like to ask her some questions, too," Javier said.

"Were you having sex with Rod?" I asked.

"I wouldn't call it sex."

"What would you call it?"

"Just, you know, messing around. I mean, he had AIDS, right? I wasn't going to have, like, *real* sex with him. I have a wife."

"She didn't mind your messing around with him?" Javier asked.

"No. She thought it was hot as long as I was careful. Okay?" Javier looked over his shoulder at me and asked, "Is that all you want to know?"

"Yeah, I'm done."

He eased off Allan, allowing him to get off the hood of the

car. Allan stood up, hands still on his junk and looked around the sidewalk.

"Have either of you seen my thong?"

"No," we said in unison.

"Damn. Those things are expensive. You wouldn't think so, but they are."

13

I DREAMED I WAS SITTING AT A VERY LARGE, VERY ROUND table. Across from me were Jeffer, my mother and Javier O'Shea. Javier was dressed in a suit of armor and looked incredible sexy even though only a tiny bit of his face was visible. My mother wore a kind of dunce cap with a veil attached to the tip. Jeffer was in some kind of purple brocade with a golden crown upon his head. He opened his mouth and began to sing, "If Ever I Should Leave You."

I bolted upright in bed and said, "King—"

The song was actually playing in the living room. I got out of bed and went out there. When my mother saw me come into the room, she said, "I hope I didn't wake you. I saw that you had *Camelot*. It's my favorite musical. I thought it would be nice to hear—"

"King—"

"Yes dear, it's about King Arthur."

"No, um, Kingdon, Kingle, Kingsford, Kingston, I think that's it, yeah it is. Kingston Investments."

"Oh you remembered! That's wonderful."

I hurried over to my desk and took the phone book out of the bottom drawer. I flipped through to the yellow pages and looked up investment firms. When I got there, I skimmed the listings until I found Kingston Investments. It was at 1680 Vine

Street. Suite 1104. We'd have to go there first thing Monday morning.

"What time is your flight tomorrow?"

"A little after one."

If we went at nine and got out of there at ten we'd likely be at the airport by eleven, which was plenty of time for my mother to check-in—

Then I noticed something. The loveseat was made up for sleeping, with sheets and a blanket, and one of the pillows from my bed. My bed where I'd woken up.

"Why didn't you sleep in my bed? I wanted to sleep out here."

"I put you in your own bed. I thought it best. You were very tipsy last night."

"I was?"

"Yes dear. After you and Javier chased down that stripper, he bought everyone a shot of tequila. I didn't want mine so you—"

"Oh my God. Was I embarrassing?" In front of Javier. In front of my mother!

"Well, you did get a little handsy with the stripper."

"No, that wasn't my fault. Louis gave me a five dollar bill and so Allan or Zeus grabbed my—"

"Not that stripper, dear, the one who came on later."

"Oh."

"I think his name was Adonis. Well, not his real name, obviously. His professional name. At least, I assume it wasn't his real name. It would be a very awkward real name."

A vague memory of a stunningly attractive guy with bronzed skin came flooding back. "Oh God."

"Do you ever go to places like that by yourself?"

"No." I didn't, but I also wouldn't tell her if I did.

"That's good. I think you're much more likely to meet a nice young man at a place like New York, New York. Do you go there by yourself?"

"Mostly I go with Marc and Louis."

"Oh, you should go by yourself every once in a while. Marc and Louis are wonderful, but you'll never meet anyone if you spend all your time with them. I think Leon is interesting, but apparently you don't, so that's fine. Of course, if you bide your time Javier will be available again."

"Mom, I don't think we should be talking about this."

"All right, then get in the shower and get ready."

"Get ready for what?"

"We're going out for brunch. Someplace called Millie's? We decided last night."

"I don't remember agreeing to that."

"You didn't agree to it. You suggested it."

"Oh. Great."

WE MET Marc and Louis in the courtyard. They were dressed nicely in pleated slacks and pressed shirts. I wore a pair of jeans with a rip over the knee, and a knit hat to cover my impossible hair.

"Is Millie's a lot fancier than it was three weeks ago?" I asked.

"We're leaving for the theater right after brunch," Louis explained. "*Angels in America* at the Taper. It's a marathon, we're seeing both halves in one day."

"There's a dinner break in the middle," Marc added.

"Is it a long play?" my mother asked.

"Over seven hours, I think."

"What's it about?"

"AIDS, Mormons, Roy Cohen," Louis replied.

"Do Mormons get AIDS? I mean, more than other people?"

"No," Marc said. "I think it's more about religion in general rather than just Mormons."

"Oh."

As we started down the red stairs, Detective Amberson was climbing up them. He looked like one of those GQ spreads, where they put well-dressed men in unlikely situations. He stopped a few steps below us.

"I understand you were at The Hawk last night questioning

our prime suspect."

"Prime suspect for what?" I asked. "Rod Brusco died of an overdose and his mother tried to kill herself two days later. Isn't that the official line?"

As soon as it was out of my mouth I realized how confrontational it sounded. Where were my inhibitions? Was I still drunk? Nevertheless, I wasn't surprised by the cold, angry look Amberson gave me in return.

"I'm under no obligation to keep you informed of the progress of our investigation."

"Then why are you here?" Oh crap, that was confrontational too.

"I told you to stay out of this."

"But you also told me there wasn't a *this*. So what exactly am I supposed to stay out of?"

"Don't go near Allan Hinsdale again. Any of you."

"Great. We won't."

He gave us one of his patented dirty looks and turned to go back down the stairs. Before he took a step, I said, "He's not the prime suspect. Not anymore."

"What do you mean by that?"

"I mean, we found out who the Kileys are."

"The Kileys? What are you talking about?"

"I told you I overheard—they want to rent Rod's apartment."

"Well, it's available."

"We also found out that Rod sold his insurance."

"It's called viatical insurance," Louis added.

"He sold it through an investment firm called—"

"What are you talking about? What does insurance have to do with this?"

"It's motive. Whoever bought his policy wouldn't get paid until—"

"Are you not listening to me? I keep telling you to stay out of this. You're wasting my time and I hate wasting time."

"We talked to Rod's ex."

"Yeah, I talked to him, but he didn't say anything about

insurance."

"He didn't actually know about the insurance—"

"Then why are you talking about him?"

"Rod went to a support group."

"A support group that sells insurance?"

"No, a support group for people with HIV."

"Rod Brusco had AIDS? That's not in the autopsy."

"Oh."

"Not that it's any of your business, but we found a suspicious deposit of twenty-five hundred dollars cash to the Hinsdales' account."

"That's from the Kileys. They wanted to know when Rod's apartment was available. They lied to the Kileys telling them they were the managers."

"That doesn't make sense. Twenty-five hundred to tell them when an apartment comes available? There's no rental crisis in L.A. It's easy to rent a place."

"I know. They used to live in number 17. Their daughter wants to be an actress and they want her to live in the apartment they first lived in. I guess it's for luck or something."

"Okay, well that's an even stupider story. It didn't occur to you that Allan Hinsdale might be lying? Somebody gave him twenty-five hundred—"

"A thousand. He thinks it was a thousand. His wife probably lied to him about the rest." And if he let his wife do the banking, like my parents always had, he'd never even see the bank statement.

"The Hinsdales were paid for something. Probably holding a pillow over their next door neighbor's face. See how that's logical?"

Reluctantly, I said, "Yeah."

"But you want me to believe that he was given the money to tell someone when a particular apartment was empty. You see how that's not logical?"

I could, actually, but I refused to say it out loud. Were we wrong? Were we making a mistake? Wait, it wasn't that Allan and his wife didn't have a motive, it's that someone else had a better one. Unless Amberson was right and Allan had been lying to us. The Kileys might be the investors, and if they paid—

The detective turned and walked down the steps. I was frustrated. I knew that if he just listened to me with an open mind we'd be able to figure this out. He probably knew things we didn't, and we definitely knew things he didn't. If we put them all—

"You're screwing this up," I said.

He turned around and looked at me long and hard.

"That's strike two. You have one more and I'm throwing your ass in jail."

MILLIE'S WAS a favorite spot of ours since it was a two-minute drive down the hill to Sunset. Of course, it was usually ten minutes to find parking and twenty minutes in line to get a table. But the fact that it was close made it a number one choice.

It had been there forever and only sat about thirty people, inside and out. That morning we were lucky that Leon had arrived ahead of us and gotten one of the three tables on the sidewalk. The fact that the table was meant for four didn't stop the five of us from squeezing in around it.

As we sat down at the table with Leon, Marc said, "That awful detective came by to harass us again."

"Us? Me. He barely looked at you guys."

"But when he did…" Marc mimicked a shiver.

"He does have an intimidating way about him," my mother said. "I suppose that's useful when it comes to criminals, but we're hardly that."

"You must be onto something," Leon said. "He wouldn't bother with you if you weren't."

"I don't think he'd agree with you. He wants us to stay away from their suspect, Allan Hinsdale."

"Well, I guess that's easy enough," he said. "Did you remember the name of that investment firm?"

"I did. It's Kingston Investments. They're on Hollywood and Vine. We'll go first thing in the morning."

"Oh no, darling," Leon said. "We should go today."

"It's Sunday. They're closed."

"Yes, I assumed that."

"Then why—"

"Are you saying what I think you're saying?" Louis asked.

"Absolutely, we should break in and steal the information we need."

The waitress came over; we'd had her before. She had flat black hair cut into a long pageboy a la Bettie Page and wore a gingham blouse. Snapping her gum, she said, "We have mimosas." But the way she crinkled her nose meant that they either weren't very good or she was annoyed by having to serve them. We all ordered coffee.

Once the waitress walked away, Marc said, "Are you seriously suggesting we break into an office on Hollywood Boulevard and steal Rod's file to find out who his investor is?"

"Wait a minute. What if there's more than one investor?" Louis asked. "What if it's one of those financial things where they chop everything up and nothing's owned by just one person?"

"Well, in that case we should be looking very closely at the investment firm," Leon replied. "Maybe the broker guaranteed his investors a particular return and the only way to get it was to kill Rod. So they—"

"Oh my God, what if they killed other boys? What if Rod's not the only one?" my mother asked. She'd obviously seen too many Charlton Heston movies.

"I don't know," I said. "It's not a very good address. I get the impression the company is doing private exchanges. Not the big, multi-investor kind of thing. If they were doing that, they'd be over in Brentwood or Beverly Hills."

"That's actually a good point," Louis said. "A good investment broker would never rent an office in Hollywood."

"Well, either way," Leon said. "We won't know until we get a look at Rod's file."

"Could we go late tonight?" Marc asked. "We have theater tickets."

"Oh that's right," Leon said. "*Angels in America*? I hear it's life-changing, though probably not as life-changing as committing burglary."

"We should be home by eleven-thirty. We could do it then."

"Louis, what about the break?" Marc asked. "It's almost two hours and it's Sunday so there won't be a lot of traffic."

"You want to commit a burglary during intermission?" I asked.

"It's not intermission. It's a dinner break."

The waitress came back with a tray of coffees. We sat quietly while she passed them out, then put the empty tray on a stand.

"You wanna order?" she asked, still snapping her gum.

I started to shake my head, but Louis said, "Yes, we're on a bit of a timetable. I'll have two eggs over easy, bacon and wheat toast."

"And I'll have the banana walnut pancakes with sausage,'" Marc ordered.

Leon asked for the huevos rancheros and I decided on the mushroom omelet with sourdough toast.

"Oh my, it's my turn, isn't it?" my mother said. "Well, all right then. I guess I'll have the California Benedict, since I'm visiting."

The waitress picked up the menus and walked away.

"Where were we?" Leon asked, sipping his coffee.

"*You* were fantasizing about breaking into Kingston Investments," I said as I sugared mine.

"It's not a fantasy," Leon insisted. "We're going to do it."

"No, I don't think so," I said with as much finality as I could muster.

"If the five of us can't figure out how to commit a simple burglary and get away with it, then what good are we?"

"I don't think they'll have tons of security. Not at that location," Marc said.

"Can anyone pick a lock?" Louis asked.

There was a long pause. "Really?" Leon said. "Were none of

you ever delinquent?"

"I can pick a lock with a bobby pin," my mother admitted.

"You can?!" My chin nearly hit the table.

"I don't mean to brag, but I can. I'm actually good at it too. When Noah was an infant I kept forgetting my keys and locking myself out of the house. Well, his father hit the roof. We couldn't afford a locksmith to come and let me in all the time and he couldn't leave the office. So there I was; I had to do something."

"So you learned to pick a lock," Leon said.

"But you haven't picked a lock in decades," I pointed out.

"It's not something you forget."

Really? I wondered. You forget your keys but not how to pick a lock?

"I tried to open a door with a credit card once," Marc said. "I had to call and get them to send me a new one."

"How would we even get into the building?" I asked. "I'm sure there will be a security guard."

"I'll think of a story," Leon said.

"Four of us are going to look suspicious."

"Five," my mother said. I frowned.

"Actually, I think it should just be me and Angie," Leon said.

"No."

"I need her to pick the lock. She needs me to get in."

"She's got a flight tomorrow. She can't get arrested."

"We're not going to get arrested. And even if we did get arrested, we just have to get her on the plane. The LAPD is not going to extradite her from Ohio over an office burglary."

"Michigan."

"Same difference."

"If it's just going to be Leon and my mom, then you guys don't need to be there," I said hoping the whole thing would fall apart.

"Oh no, we have to be there," Marc said.

"We need to at least aid and abet," Louis agreed.

And then I gave up all hope.

14

AFTER BRUNCH, MY MOTHER AND I DROVE TO ROD'S apartment. As I made the turn off Cahuenga, I noticed his car was gone. I suppose that wasn't surprising. The police might have taken it somewhere to process it for evidence. Or sitting there with its window broken it could easily have been stolen. On the other hand, it might have been repossessed. Who knew when Rod had made his last payment?

We parked on the same side street we'd been parking on all weekend. Things seemed quiet. With Joanne's key, we let ourselves into the building. Eddie was in the courtyard hosing down the patio area around the pool, with him was his older boy. The boy wore a plastic fireman's helmet and held a squirt gun almost as big as he was. He raised the gun and aimed.

"Jorge!" his father yelled. It was too late though; a blast of water hit me in the middle of the chest. I was a goner.

"I'm really sorry," Eddie said, pulling the plastic toy out of his son's hands. The boy started to cry immediately, causing his father to ask, "What have I told you?"

The boy said something through his tears, though I couldn't understand what. I assumed it might have been "Don't squirt strangers."

"He's never learned the word 'no.'" Eddie said. "He takes after his mother that way."

"He's darling," my mother said.

I probably should have jumped in and said something nice about the boy as well, but I was too damp.

"Say, um, do you know when Joanne's going to come back to pack up the apartment?" No, 'how is she?' or 'give her my best.'

"She's still in the hospital," my mother said.

"Oh, yes, of course. She will get better though, won't she?"

"Yes, she should be out very soon."

"Oh, that's good to hear. Tell her I said to get well."

Finally, I thought. We smiled a goodbye and walked toward number 17. When we got inside, I went directly to the kitchen and ripped off a few sheets of paper towels. I applied them to my chest.

"Is it just me or does he seem awfully worried about when Joanne's going to be out of here?"

"He's losing money. That must be frightening with three small children."

I didn't say anything because I'd already sat down at Rod's desk and was flipping through his Pendaflex files.

"I can't find Rod's insurance form. You know, the one that Joanne found that listed her as beneficiary."

"Maybe it's in her purse," my mother said, as she walked over to Joanne's large purse, which sat on the coffee table in a lump. She opened it and looked in. "No, it's not here. Do you think the police took it?"

"Somebody broke into Rod's car and took the folder from Kingston Investments. Maybe that person got in here too."

"Noah," my mother said, her voice grave. "Joanne's gun isn't here." She stood and looked around the room. "Maybe it's by the bed."

"No, Mom, she slept out here, remember?"

"Oh that's right. Do you think the police have it?"

"They might. I mean, they can take anything that's evidence."

"But it's not evidence."

"Do you think it's registered? They could take it if she didn't have the right paperwork."

She reached back into the purse and took out Joanne's red leather wallet. After a moment she said, "Oh, she has a registration card. It says she can carry a gun."

I looked over her shoulder. "In Indiana. I don't know if California recognizes that."

"So the police could have taken it?"

"If it was still here, yes."

She looked over at Joanne's suitcase which sat open on the leather chair. "Should we just bring everything? Or should I just bring her a few changes of clothing?"

"This apartment doesn't feel very secure. Why don't we bring everything."

"Look in the bathroom for her makeup case."

I walked through the bedroom to the bathroom. The bedroom looked pretty much as my mother and I had left it. Joanne probably hadn't come into the room at all and there wasn't much reason for the police to snoop around in there a second time.

In the bathroom, it was a different story. Her makeup case sat on the vanity. It seemed obvious that the police had gone through it—and possibly someone else. Everything was jumbled up into a big mess. Joanne hardly seemed the organized type, but no woman kept her things in this kind of chaos. The medicine cabinet was open. I imagined whichever police officer opened it was disappointed to find only vitamins, just as I had been. Now I understood them.

Closing the case, I carried it out into the living room. My mother was in the middle of refolding everything in Joanne's suitcase. I felt a little guilty about the condition of the case.

"They really did make a mess of everything," my mother said.

There was a knock on the door, followed by the door opening a crack and Number 5 sticking his head in. "Hello."

We said 'hello' and then he said, "I saw you come in. How is Rod's mom doing?"

"She's going to be fine," my mother said. "We're going to see her in a few minutes."

"Any idea what happened? I mean, did someone really try to poison her? Who would do that?"

"The same person who killed Rod," I said.

"But he—wasn't that an overdose?"

"Did you see him take any drugs at the party?"

"No, there were a lot of people there."

"Was anyone doing drugs?"

He glanced at my mother. "No, no drugs. Just marijuana."

"Who brought the marijuana?"

"Rod."

"Rod? I thought you said he used people for drugs."

Number 5 shrugged. "I didn't say he paid for the pot. Who knows where he got it?"

"Did he share?" I asked.

"I guess. I didn't notice, but people do."

"Did you see anyone give Rod the marijuana?" my mother asked. "Or any packages?"

He shook his head. "I'm pretty sure he came with the dope. Rod was the one who was a pothead. We went to him when we wanted something." Which might explain what Rod was living on after he ran out of money. "If you had a better source you avoided him though. He tended to overcharge and he'd always ask you for a joint or two."

"Who was at the party?" As soon as I asked, I remembered that Javier was going to come by and get a list from Allan. I wondered if he'd already been there.

"Oh my God, like tons of people."

"People who live in the building?" my mother wanted to know.

"Yeah, there were a lot of people from the building. But mostly there were Allan's stripper friends and some of his friends from an acting class. There were a couple of girls who looked like they were friends of Tabitha's."

"Did anyone behave suspiciously?"

"No."

"There were no arguments or fights or anything like that?"

"Sure there were. It was a party."

"Who was fighting?" my mother asked, like she might discipline someone.

"Well, I'm not sure I'd call it a fight, but Eddie did make a crack about Rod's being behind in his rent."

"Did he?"

"I mean, it was over before it even started really. Eddie's wife said something in his ear and after that he didn't say anything else."

I was missing something, but exactly what I wasn't sure. Then something struck me. "Was your boyfriend at the party?"

"My boyfriend?"

"Yes, the one Rod tried to help himself to, remember?"

"Oh, well, we broke up."

"Over Rod?"

"Among other things."

"Did *you* fight with Rod?"

"No. I would never fight over Rod Brusco's sloppy seconds. Wait, are you accusing me of something?"

"I'm just asking."

"I only came over here to find out if Joanne's okay. I don't think I deserve to be accused of something." He turned and walked out of the apartment.

"He's right you know," my mother said. "He didn't deserve to be accused of anything."

"I didn't accuse him."

"I know he had a reason to kill Rod, but he didn't have any reason to try to kill Joanne, did he?"

"No. None that I can see."

"I think we're ready," she said, closing the suitcase. I steeled myself then picked up the suitcase. My mother took the makeup case. We left the apartment and went down the stairs. I stopped and decided to check something out.

Setting down the suitcase, I ran up the stairs to number 16 and knocked. After a moment, Tabitha came to the door. Her nose and eyes were red. She glared at me but didn't say hello.

"Is Allan here?"

"No. He's not."

"He was supposed to make a list of who was at your party for one of the detectives. The detective was going to come by this—"

"Yeah, he came by. But there's no list. Allan didn't come home last night, okay?"

"Okay. Do you know where he is?"

"Gone. I think he's in Palm Springs. He has a 'friend' there."

"Oh. You wouldn't be willing to make a list of who was—"

"No," she said, slamming the door in my face. I assumed that was the same answer she'd given Javier.

THE PSYCHIATRIC WARD was on the top floor of the hospital. We gave Joanne's luggage to a nurse at the duty desk. Presumably, she'd look through it and take anything out that wasn't safe for a psychiatric patient to have. The nurse did take a quick look through Joanne's purse and then said we could give that to her. Handing it back, she told us to go down the hall and wait in the lounge. She'd let Joanne know we were there to see her.

The lounge was a small sofa sitting in front of a window at the end of the hall. There was a coffee table and two spindly wire chairs. Magazines covered the table: *Time, Newsweek, People, Us Weekly*. I hoped we wouldn't have to be there long enough to read any of them.

"It's terrible that that detective is making her stay in here," my mother said. "It should be illegal to do something like that."

I had to be honest, though, so I said, "This is the safest place for her if someone's trying to kill her."

"You think they'll try again?"

"We don't want to find out the hard way, do we?"

A few minutes later, Joanne came down the hallway wearing a hospital gown. My mother gave her a big hug while I hung back. Was I supposed to hug her too? I didn't want to. I barely knew her. Fortunately, the moment passed when my mother handed Joanne her purse.

"It's so nice to see you up and around," she said.

"I feel like a punching bag," Joanne said as she sat down on one of the wire chairs. Immediately she began digging through her purse. After a moment she asked, "Did you take my gun out of here?"

"They wouldn't let you have it in here," I said, deciding not to tell her we couldn't find it.

"Have they said when they're going to let you go?" my mother asked.

"Tomorrow, I think." Joanne took a long breath. "Different young women keep coming in and asking me if I'm depressed. I tell them, 'Of course I'm depressed, my son just died.' But that just seems to rev them up. They want to know if I'm thinking about harming myself. I don't want to harm myself, I want to harm the person who killed my son."

"They're just doing their jobs, Joanne."

"I know that, but isn't it also their job to listen to me?"

"They must be listening if they're going to let you out tomorrow."

Joanne considered that. "Maybe you're right. But my God, the thought of spending another day in here... They have me in a room with a woman who's completely bonkers. Keeps telling me she's Jackie Kennedy. And they don't look at bit alike."

"Have the police been in to talk to you?" I asked.

"I think I spoke to someone when I first got here, but it's all pretty hazy."

"They haven't been back?" That seemed odd. If she was hazy the first time they spoke to her, they—Detective Amberson—should have come back and asked her the same questions again.

"Have they found anything out? Do they even believe Rod was murdered?"

"I think they do, yes. They have a prime suspect, but I think they're wrong about him."

"What about the people next door?" she asked.

"That's who I mean. Amberson seemed sure the guy next door did it."

"But I think he did do it. He had to have."

I couldn't explain our theory without telling her that Rod was HIV positive and I did *not* want to do that.

"It's possible that Rod may have made some bad investments."

"Really? That's not like him. I mean, he played the stock market but was really good at it. He told me—" She stopped. Disappointment played across her face. I think she was beginning to realize her son didn't always tell the truth.

I decided to give my mother a bit of time on her own with Joanne by saying, "I need to find a pay phone and check on the store."

"All right, we'll stay right here," my mother said.

"The phones are down the hall just after the nurse's station," Joanne told me. Then to my mother she said, "They make you beg for quarters and then ask who you're calling."

Poor Joanne, I thought, *it must be awful to be in a place like this when you don't need to be.* Actually, that wasn't right. It was worse to be in here if you needed to be. Which meant it was a horrible place to be no matter what.

Shoving the thought from my mind, I walked down the hall to the pay phone. No one asked who I was calling.

Mikey picked up the phone. "Pinx Video, this is Michael."

Michael? When had he started that?

"Mikey this is Noah."

"Oh, hi!"

"I just want to check on things."

"Things are quiet. It'll pick up later, I'm sure."

On a holiday weekend people came in before and after, but not very much during. Wednesday night had been busy with family types picking up kids' videos to distract their children, and single types picking up pornos to distract themselves. Sunday night will be busy, as they'll return the videos they rented.

"I'm sorry I haven't been around more."

"Don't be silly. We all hope you're having a wonderful time with your mother."

"Oh, um, I am," I said. And I was; sort of.

"That police officer stopped by a little while ago."

"Which police officer?"

"The good-looking one."

"Oh. Him." He probably wanted to tell me that Allan had run off without leaving a list. At least, I hoped that's what he wanted to tell me. There wasn't more to last night than I remembered, was there? Well, yes, there was. My conversation with my mother that morning had made that clear.

Oh God. He stopped by rather than calling. That seemed serious. Or wait, maybe he did call. I hadn't checked my messages yet.

"He didn't say what he wanted, did he?"

"No. He just asked if you were coming in and I said I didn't think so, then he rented *The Great Mouse Detective* and left."

"Okay, thanks. I'm not going to be home for a while. If you need anything leave me a message there. I'll check it every so often."

"Don't worry. I've got everything under control."

I dialed my home number and waited for my machine to pick up. When it did, I dialed 1-1-1 into the phone and my messages began to play. There were two.

The first had come in sometime Friday and I'd just ignored it. It was from my doctor's office reminding me I had an appointment Monday afternoon at one o'clock. That shouldn't be any problem. I'd go after I dropped my mother off at the airport around eleven.

The second message was the one I wanted. "Hi, Noah. This Javier O'Shea." Did he think I knew a lot of Javiers? "I went by Allan Hinsdale's apartment this morning. He's gone. Apparently in Palm Springs somewhere. His wife wouldn't be more specific. Amberson is going to have a fit when he finds out. He's left me three messages. Amberson, I mean, not Hinsdale. Anyway, the smart thing for me to do would be to tell you to stop whatever you're doing—and I know you're doing something, and you're not going to stop even if I tell you to, so let's do the stupid thing. Call me and tell me whatever you find out."

I thought about calling him, but I didn't really know much more than he did. Well, I did know the name of the investment company that arranged the purchase of Rod's life insurance. And I knew that we were going to burglarize them. That right there was a reason not to call him back until that evening—after we'd committed a crime.

I walked away from the pay phone and went back down to my mother and Joanne. My mother was holding Joanne's hand and speaking in a soft voice. When she saw me she smiled and said, "Joanne's a little tired, so we're going to leave her. They should be letting her out in the morning, so hopefully we'll be able to come by and say goodbye."

She kissed Joanne on the cheek and said "Get some rest."

"That's all I do is sleep," Joanne said.

My mother hooked me by the arm and led me toward the elevator. When we got there she pressed one.

"You told her, didn't you? You told her Rod was HIV positive."

"Yes. Someone was going to eventually. I thought it would be better if it was me."

"I don't think he would have wanted her to know."

"I understand. But she needs to know. It may be part of why he was killed. We can't keep it from her. I just didn't want that horrible Amberson fellow telling her. Did you want that?"

"No."

The elevator arrived and we got in.

"I'm sure you'll see that I was right."

"Being right doesn't always make things better."

15

The Observatory is easy to get to. You just find the entrance to Griffith Park on Los Feliz—either one—and follow the road up. It was cloudy and cool, which was unfortunate since it's a spectacular place to go on a beautiful day. Still, there were a lot of people up there. The parking lot was full, so I ended up parking along Observatory Road behind a tiny Japanese Jeep.

I was still a bit annoyed with my mother about telling Joanne Rod's secret. She was right, of course, but that just made it worse. I thought a little sightseeing might make a good penance.

We walked up the road to the wide, white building with three dark green domes. Stopping, we looked over the Astronomer's Monument, which was a white Art Deco tower held up by statues of six historically important astronomers. My mother slipped her hand into the crook of my elbow as we read the names of the scientists: Hipparchus, Copernicus, Galileo, Kepler, Newton and Herschel. I barely knew who any of them were and certainly wasn't sure what their contributions had been. Well, I think Galileo proved that the Earth was moving and not the stars—though, actually they moved too, just not around a stationary us. And Newton had something to do with gravity. I decided to trust the sculpture that they were all important. After we briefly looked at the sundial, we walked up the sidewalk to the Observatory itself.

"See, that's where they filmed *Rebel Without a Cause*," I said, pointing at the steps in front of us.

"I think your father and I went to see that on a date. They were all such beautiful, young people," she said. I knew she meant James Dean, Sal Mineo and Natalie Wood. "And they're all gone now."

I almost made a flip remark about dying young and leaving an attractive corpse, but I think all three had been pretty mangled by death.

"Noah."

"Mmm-hmmm."

"I don't want you to die."

I wished she hadn't said that. I knew what she wanted to hear. She wanted me to promise not to die, but I couldn't. So I went with the more truthful and prosaic, "Everyone dies, Mom."

"You're not everyone. You're mine."

Now she'd cornered me. "I'm going to do my best. Okay?"

"Well, I suppose I shouldn't ask for more than that." Although I could tell she wanted to.

"Let's walk around this way and get a good look at the view. I led her to the west side of the Observatory. On the east side there was a path that led down to a place where I'd almost gotten a man—and possibly myself—killed. I decided to leave that off the tour. She already had enough to deal with.

"I'm sorry to get maudlin, dear."

"It's all right."

"Poor Joanne. It breaks my heart to see another woman lose her son. I'm not sure I can think of anything worse."

"Don't try."

"I hope it will help when we find Rod's killer."

"I think it will."

I knew I should try to talk her out of burglarizing an office later that afternoon. That would be the responsible thing to do. But—I couldn't. There was something about telling her she couldn't help her friend, that she couldn't take a risk, that just felt wrong.

"Sometimes I wonder..." she stopped. "Sometimes I wonder what it might have been like if I'd married a more interesting man than your father."

"Jeffer was an interesting man," I said without thinking.

"Yes, he was, wasn't he? I suppose I should be happy with what I had, shouldn't I?"

"It's not good to regret things you can't do anything about. It doesn't lead anywhere."

I did, sometimes, wonder what my life would have been like if I'd never met Jeffer, never fallen in love with him, never trusted—but I couldn't ever get a clear picture. The only thing I knew for sure was that it would be different and I wouldn't be where I was right now. And now was not too bad. I liked now.

It didn't mean the things Jeffer did weren't still awful, it just meant I'd made the best of things then and the bad things led me to the now I liked.

"I don't regret your father," my mother said. "And I wouldn't change a thing. Maybe you need to find a man like your father. Someone just a bit dull."

That made me smile a little. "I'll keep that in mind."

On the way home, I drove through the drive-through at In-N-Out Burger on Sunset. We saved the cheeseburgers for home, but ate the French fries on the way. It was quiet when we got there. Marc and Louis were still at the play. Leon would be there at five, and Marc and Louis would pick us up a few minutes later.

"What do you think I should wear?" my mother asked.

"Black is traditional for felonies."

"Noah, we're not cat burglars. I should probably wear slacks though. And nothing flashy. I don't want to be memorable."

I didn't think she owned anything flashy.

A bit later she came out of the bathroom in a pair of charcoal gray slacks, a beige sweater set and a strand of pearls. She looked more like a librarian than a burglar, which I suppose was the point.

A half an hour later, the sun had set and we were climbing into Marc's Infiniti. Leon had arrived moments before Marc and Louis pulled up. As Louis—who was driving—pulled away, Leon complained, "I had no idea what to wear. I know the story I want to tell the guard, but I wasn't sure how to dress the part."

"What *are* you going to tell the guard?" I asked.

"I'm not saying. I don't want to sound rehearsed."

"You don't know, do you?"

"Everything is going to be fine. I'm a studio executive, if there's one thing I know how to do it's cover my ass. There will be no repercussions from our little escapade. Trust me."

I have to say, I didn't. But there didn't seem to be much I could do to stop whatever was about to happen. I sat back in the seat, closed my eyes and wished I were somewhere else. That didn't work either.

"How is the show?" Leon asked.

"Oh my God, it's amazing," Marc said.

"It's much funnier than I expected," Louis said.

They chatted about the show for nearly the whole fifteen minutes it took to get to Hollywood and Vine. Marc recounted much of the first act, which sounded a bit confusing. I had the feeling it was one of those things you had to see to 'get.' We avoided the freeway; traffic would be picking up again since people were returning to wherever they were when the holiday began three days before. And then we were there.

Kingston Investments was located on the eleventh floor of a hundred-year-old, fifteen-story, yellow brick building with a kind of ornamental cap on top. There were shops on the first floor: a wig store, a mobile phone place, and, the most upscale, a coffee shop in the corner storefront. The building's lobby was on the Vine side.

We drove around the building twice, casing the joint, I guess you'd say. Louis pulled over to the curb on the west side of Vine.

"Are you ready, Angie?" Leon asked.

"Oh yes. I have a brand new package of bobby pins in my purse."

"Then we're set to go," Leon said, opening the door and jumping out of the car.

I grabbed my mom's hand before she slid across the seat. "Be careful."

"I will be. Don't worry."

And then she jumped out of the car too. We watched quietly as Leon and my mother jaywalked across Vine and onto the sidewalk half a block down from the lobby. I could see that my mother was looking at the stars on the sidewalk as she hurried to keep up with Leon. Well, I guess that counted as sightseeing.

Louis pulled the car forward fifty feet so that we could see directly into the well-lit lobby. There was a bored, black guard of around sixty sitting at a veneered, chest-high desk in the middle of the marble lobby. On one side was a directory on a black letter board. Somewhere behind the desk were the elevators.

Leon and my mother walked into the lobby. The guard barely registered that they were there. Was he really so bored that even the surprise appearance of Leon and my mother didn't shake him? Leon was clearly telling a story, long and elaborate. The guard was not reacting. I suspected Leon was telling bigger and bigger lies trying to get him to react.

Suddenly, the guard put a clipboard on the shelf in front of him. Leon pulled out his wallet while my mother was opening her purse.

"Oh my God, they're showing him their IDs. That's insane."

"I'm sure Leon knows what he's doing."

"We might as well call the cops on ourselves."

Now they were signing the clipboard.

"Oh my God. He's got their names. Their real names."

"I see that," Louis said.

"That's not good."

"I'm sure Leon knows what he's doing," Marc said.

"Why? Why are you sure?"

"Um, well—" he trailed off, uncertain of what to say next.

"They're getting in," Marc said.

"But he knows their *names*. They wrote them down!"

We watched as Leon and my mother walked to the elevators. The guard took the clipboard and brought it back down to the desk in front of him. I wondered if he had security monitors in front of him, and if so, where were the cameras aimed? He might have a couple of screens in front of him, but he couldn't possibly have one for each floor. They probably just recorded the front and back doors.

I could just see their heads. My mother looked calm and comfortable. She chatted with Leon casually as they waited for the elevator. It finally came and they got inside. Then they were gone. I couldn't see them anymore.

"I'm going to go get a coffee," Marc said.

"What? Is that a good idea?" I asked. "We're the getaway car, after all."

"Oh, they'll be gone for a while."

I hoped a while didn't mean five to ten.

"I'll have a cafe latte," Louis said.

"Noah?"

"I couldn't." My stomach was already squeezed into a tight fist. Coffee would have destroyed me. I should never have let my mother come to Los Angeles. I should have gone home to Grand Rapids. I should be sitting in a corner at The Apartment Lounge right now looking at old high school friends wondering what to say to them if they recognized me. Instead, my mother was committing a felony. And so was I.

Marc got out and ran over to the coffee place.

"Don't worry, everything will be fine."

"What do you think they said to the guard?" I asked.

"Something that made him think it was okay to let them in, obviously."

"She can't get arrested. That would be horrible."

"Everything's going to be fine."

"What if someone's up there? What if this guy works weekends?"

"I'm sure Leon will find something to say. You'd be surprised the things he can talk his way out of."

"Oh God."

I was tempted to curl up into a fetal position on the back-seat. I doubted that would make Louis happy though, so I kept sitting there with my eyes riveted on the lobby.

"Hang in there," he said. "It's going to be okay."

'They're on the eleventh floor by now."

"Probably."

I imagined them walking down a hallway, looking for the right office, finding it. My mother would be taking out a bobby pin, bending it to slip into the lock. Or at least I thought that's what she might be doing, I really had no idea how to pick a lock.

Louis cleared his throat and said, "The Vine Street Bar and Grill is on the next block. Last year Marc and I saw Anita O'Day."

I wasn't sure who she was, so I said, "Oh yeah?"

"She was great. We'll play you her album sometime."

"Uh-huh. Do you think they're in yet?"

"No, I don't think so. Try to relax. Let's take a ride around the block so we don't look too suspicious."

Of course, circling the block and then parking illegally were suspicious in themselves. Still, I tried to relax. I really did. This was not a great part of town. There were obvious runaways on the street, homeless old ladies pushing shopping carts, and the people who preyed on runaways and homeless ladies. Hardly the part of town you'd come to if you wanted to make a stable investment. I wondered if my mother and Leon would have to flip through many files to find Rod's. It seemed unlikely they would. We got stuck at a couple of lights and it took longer to get around the block than you'd think. When we got back, Marc was standing on the side-walk where we'd been parked before. He had two large, paper coffee cups in his hands. Louis pulled up in front of him.

Marc set the coffee on the roof for a moment while he opened his door. Then he held out Louis' coffee to him. Louis took it. Then he climbed in with his coffee. They sipped for a moment.

"I was telling Noah about seeing Anita O'Day down the street."

"She was great. Do you like jazz, Noah?"

"Oh, I don't know, sometimes." I couldn't talk about jazz, not when my heart was beating like "Flight of the Bumblebee," whoever that was by. "They should be back by now, don't you think?"

"It's fine," Louis said.

I studied the guard. He looked just as bored as before. That was good. That meant there hadn't been any alarms going off. He hadn't had to frantically call the police.

Marc and Louis sipped their coffee drinks while I chewed my lip. I wanted to ask again if they shouldn't be back already, but I didn't. Louis would just tell me again that it was all—

And then Leon and my mother were coming out of the elevator. They waved at the guard and said something, presumably 'good night.' He smiled back at them. Actually smiled.

They came out onto the sidewalk and then, after looking both ways, jaywalked across Vine again. Leon opened the door for my mother and she climbed in.

"Oh dear, that was exhilarating. I feel twenty years younger."

"What took so long? You took forever," I said.

"We had to wait for the copy machine to warm up," Leon said. He shut the door and Louis drove off.

"Copy machine?"

"Yes. We copied Rod's file. We didn't want anyone to know we'd been in there. No one will ever know we were there."

"The guard knows. We saw you show your ID."

"Don't worry. I told him I was a producer who'd just rented in the building and that I wanted to show my mother the view from my office before she went back to Memphis. My office is on a different floor, by the way. Angie was wonderful."

"Oh, I barely said a word."

"Yes, but you delivered your line perfectly."

"What did you say, Angie?" Marc asked.

"As we were leaving, I said, 'Y'all have a good night.'"

"Oh my God," I said.

"So, what's in the file?" Marc wanted to know. "Did you read it while you were copying it?"

My mother opened her purse, saying, "Yes. We did—"

"It's Eddie, isn't it?" I said. "The landlord."

"How did you know that?"

"He said he was in San Diego the night of the murder, but he wasn't. He was in Hollywood at the party. I figured he had to have a good reason to lie."

"It doesn't make sense though," Marc pointed out. "Rod had all that money before he moved into The Pagoda."

"Eddie must have decided giving him a place to live was a good way to keep an eye on him," my mother said.

"Or a good way to make sure he died." I replied.

16

ON THE WAY BACK TO THE APARTMENT, I LOOKED through the file Leon and my mother had copied. There were almost ten pages. Most of them were a boilerplate contract between Rod and the Castellons, including the signature page. The final page was a letter from Rod's doctor saying he wasn't likely to live for two years. The letter was dated October 1989. More than three years ago.

The front page was a sheet summarizing the basics: names, addresses, phone numbers and amounts. Eddie and his wife had paid $180,000 for Rod's quarter of a million dollar policy. They stood to gain seventy thousand dollars.

"I was so surprised when I saw Eddie's name. He seemed so nice," my mother said.

"Okay. What do we do now?" I asked, as Louis pulled up in front of our apartment building.

"Well, we need to go back to the Taper," he said.

"I actually have a date in about an hour. Noah, why don't you call the detective working the case and tell him what we found out?"

"Detective Amberson?" I gave a little thought to what that might be like and then said, "Oh my God, we can't."

"Why can't we? We know who did it," my mother said.

"We can't tell Amberson how we found out though. He'll want to know how we know and we can't tell him we stole it."

"Wait a minute," Leon said. "Just call Javier. Tell him. He'll figure out how to get this information to Amberson."

"Guys, we have to hurry," Louis said.

"Oh sure," I said, opening the door to get out.

"We'll stop by after the show to find out how things turn out," Marc said through his window as Louis pulled away. Leaving me, my mother and Leon on the curb.

I had to go inside and call Javier. I wasn't looking forward to it. I couldn't tell him how we got the information. He'd probably be tempted to arrest me. Still, calling him was probably our best shot at getting the information to where it belonged.

We said goodbye to Leon. My mother gave him a big hug and they joked about being burglary buddies. Then he walked over to his car and drove off. We went upstairs and I beeped Javier.

As I hung up, I asked my mother, "Were you scared?"

"Terrified. But it was the good terrified."

I hadn't known that terror came in good and bad.

"You should have worn gloves," I said, suddenly thinking of fingerprints.

"Oh stop. No one will ever know we were in there."

"You turned off the Xerox machine?"

"Yes, we did. It's sweet of you to worry, but it's all fine."

Just then, the phone rang. I picked it up.

"You called?"

"Hi. Um, listen, we need to talk."

"Yes, I was thinking that would be nice."

"Oh, no. I mean, sure, but that's not… We know who killed Rod Brusco."

"You do?"

"Yes. Can you come by? I have the proof to show you."

"I can be there in ten minutes."

"Okay, thanks," I said before I hung up.

"You invited him here?" my mother asked.

"Yes."

"Do we have anything to offer him? Do you have tea bags? I could make iced tea."

"Mom, don't worry about it."

"Should we borrow something from Marc and Louis?"

"Are we going to break into their apartment?"

"I'm sure they won't mind."

I rolled my eyes. "Burglary isn't going to become a thing with you, is it?"

She frowned at me.

"We don't need to put out a big spread. We're just going to give the file to Javier and then we'll be finished. They'll arrest Eddie Castellon, then we'll have a nice breakfast somewhere tomorrow morning and I'll put you on a plane."

"And we'll pick up Joanne?"

"And we'll pick up Joanne."

"I've overstayed my welcome, haven't I?"

"No, I'd just like to get you home without an arrest record."

"I don't plan on committing anymore felonies before I go home. Okay?"

"Okay."

Then she went into my kitchen and started digging around for something that resembled food. I didn't hold much hope.

I put Don Henley on the CD player and waited for Javier to arrive. Occasionally, my mother made a sound like "hmm-mmm" or "ah-ha." I tried not to think about what she was doing. There really wasn't anything in my kitchen to speak of.

Javier arrived while Henley was deep in the heart of the matter. I opened the door and let him in.

"Thank you for coming by. I appreciate it."

"I'm on my way over to Tim's anyway." That felt weird. He'd wanted to talk to me, but he had a boyfriend so what was there to say?

"Javier, it's nice to see you again," my mother said.

"Hello, Mrs. Valentine."

I know she told him to call her Angie, but not everyone could. She didn't tell him again. Instead, she smiled and said, "Would you like a beer?"

"Thank you. I'm off duty so, yes."

"Where did you find a beer?"

"In the vegetable bin."

"Can I have one?"

She shook her head subtly. Apparently there had only been one beer in the vegetable bin. She popped into the kitchen.

"I got grilled by Amberson. He's not too happy about last night."

"We know. He stopped by this morning."

"He's this close to writing me up," Javier said holding his index finger and thumb very close together. Then got down to business. "You have something to show me?"

I sat down at the table and Javier sat next to me. I turned over the xeroxed file my mom and Leon had gotten earlier and slid it in front of him. "We need to get this to Amberson."

"What is it?"

"It's a copy of an insurance policy that Rod sold."

"He sold insurance?"

"No, he sold his own insurance. An investor or investors pay a portion of the value and when the person dies they make a profit."

"That's legal?"

My mom brought out a glass and the beer for Javier, a Miller. She set it in front of him and poured.

"Thank you," he said. "So, okay, Rod Brusco was dying?"

"He was HIV positive. Or, I guess he had AIDS. There's a doctor's letter that says he won't live two years dated three years ago."

"Poor guy. He must have been terrified."

And that was why I'd never told Javier why I wouldn't go out with him. I never wanted to tell him I was positive. I never wanted to hear that pity in his voice. I didn't want to be that poor guy. I glanced up at my mother, but I couldn't read her face. She slipped back into the kitchen.

"And his landlord is the person who bought the policy?"

"That happened before Rod moved there. I think the policy

might have had something to do with his moving into The Pagoda."

"How did you get this?"

"You don't want to know."

"I don't—" He looked at me closely. And then shook his head, presumably deciding I was right. He didn't want to know.

"Well, I can't just give this to Amberson. How did you find out about it?"

"I talked to Scottie, Rod's ex-boyfriend. He told me that Rod was HIV positive and that he went to a support group called Best Lives. A guy there named Curtis Barry told me that a lot of guys buy this kind of insurance."

He looked again at the copy. "And this Barry guy gave you the name of Kingston Investments?"

"No. There was a folder in the back of Rod's car. Kingston Investments was on it. But it was stolen out of the car. In fact, the car is gone now."

"Rod's car is gone?"

"I thought Amberson might have taken it for some reason."

"Did Rod's mother report it stolen?"

My mother sat down at the table, sliding a bowl of pinkish popcorn into the center, saying, "Joanne's in the hospital on a psychiatric hold."

"Oh, that's right. Okay, so there's no way to leave bread crumbs for Amberson. I could have called him and asked about the ex-boyfriend, but that leads to a dead-end. I could ask about the car, but that doesn't lead anywhere."

He thought for a moment, then said, "This does speak to motive. That's certainly true. But it doesn't prove he killed Rod."

"He was at the party on Wednesday night. He was right next door when Rod was killed. And he lied. He told me he was in San Diego."

"When did Rod move into that apartment?"

"Last winter."

"Which was more than a year after he signed the agreement. That's not a coincidence."

"Probably not," I said. "We don't know why he moved in, though."

"I imagine Castellon wanted to keep an eye on his investment. Seventy thousand is a lot to make over two years on a hundred and eighty thousand."

"Almost twenty percent," my mother said, munching a bit of the popcorn. She'd always been better at math than I was. "It's around twelve percent over three years."

"Which is still a good return."

"It might be more about getting the money back than what they earn," I suggested. "The Castellons look pretty crowded in their apartment."

"Where did you get this?" Javier asked again about the form.

This was going to be the hard part. "I can't tell you."

"And you want me to give this to Amberson, don't you?"

"Yes, of course."

"I'm going to have to tell him something."

"You could say it was sent to you anonymously," I suggested. I took a few pieces of popcorn from the bowl and popped them into my mouth: butter, garlic salt and—cayenne pepper? Yikes!

"Why me? Why not him? He'll know right away I got it from you."

"I guess we could send it to him," I said, wishing I had a glass of water.

"Oh no," my mother said. "That will take days. Joanne gets out of the hospital in the morning. What if Eddie tries to kill her again?"

"Anonymous tips don't carry that much weight anyway. There's always a reason they're anonymous." He gave me a suspicious look. I could tell he hated that I wasn't telling him the whole truth.

"What if Detective Amberson found it himself?" my mother asked. She was still munching popcorn as though it wasn't hot at all. "We could put it in Rod's desk and find a way to get Amberson to look for it."

"The apartment's already been searched."

"Can't it be searched again?"

"We need a reason."

That was a stumper. After a moment, I said, "I'm pretty sure someone else was in there. They took the box of chocolates for one thing. And the beneficiary form naming Joanne is missing."

"And so is her gun," my mother added.

"If we have Joanne call and ask for these things, would it trigger another search?"

"It might."

"So if we put this in Rod's desk they can find it."

"You can't just put it in Rod's desk. It would have to be somewhere they might have missed."

"You mean like taped to the bottom of a drawer," my mother said.

"That might work," Javier said, finally helping himself to some of the spicy popcorn. He was much happier with it than I was. "Mmmm, spicy," he said with a smile.

"So that's what we'll do. I'll go tape this on the bottom side of a drawer and we'll have Joanne call Amberson Monday morning."

"And then we'll cross our fingers."

———

AFTER JAVIER LEFT, we drove to Pinx for Scotch tape. When we walked in, Mickey was behind the counter. Something about that bothered me, but I didn't have time to think about what before he asked, "How was *Sister Act*?"

"We haven't had time to watch it," my mother replied. "We've been busy solving—"

"Sightseeing," I interjected.

"Oh, that's right, sightseeing," my mother repeated.

"Did you make it to Universal Studios?"

"No."

"Disneyland?"

"No—"

Knowing this could go on forever I said, "We went to The Griffith Observatory."

He waited for more sights. When then didn't come he said, "And?"

"That's it really."

Trying to be helpful, my mother said, "Oh, stop it Noah. We went to Hollywood Boulevard. I saw Donald O'Connor's star."

"Anyone else?"

"No."

"Okay."

"Oh and we went to The Hawk," my mother said proudly.

The look on Mikey's face was priceless. "You took your mother to The Hawk?"

"It's a long story."

"It would have to be."

"Look we just stopped in to grab some Scotch tape," I said. "I'll just go back to the office."

"Oh, I've got some right here." He took a dispenser out from under the counter. "Are you going to bring it back?"

"No," my mother said.

"We're not?" I asked.

"No."

"I guess we're not.

"What do you need it for?" Mikey asked.

"Photo album—" I said while my mother said, "My book fell a—"

"Wait. Why are you here?" I asked Mikey. "Isn't this Lainey's shift?"

"She couldn't make it."

"Why didn't you call me?"

"You're busy with your mom, doing—something mysterious."

"You shouldn't just do things like this, Mikey."

"It's okay. You don't have to pay me for the overtime."

"Yes, I do. For one thing it's illegal not to and for another you worked overtime. You deserve the extra money."

"But you didn't approve it."

"No, and please don't do it again." I frowned at him. "Did you at least get dinner?"

"I brought a yogurt."

I looked at my mom and said, "We need to go, but let's grab him a burrito at Taco Maria's."

"Oh you don't have to," Mikey said.

"Chicken or beef?"

"Veggie."

FORTY-FIVE MINUTES later we parked in front of The Pagoda. The air was thick with the smell of eucalyptus and it felt very dark. I could see bouncing colored lights in the first-floor apartments, people watching television. I had a nervous feeling in the pit of my stomach, but that was silly. This was easy. My mother and I had been in the apartment several times. Nothing was going to happen.

"Do you want to watch *Sister Act* when we get home?" I asked.

"Yes, we can. So Whoopie Goldberg is a nun—is that right?"

"I think she's pretending to be a nun."

"Oh, that's good. She doesn't strike me as the nun-type."

"Yeah. That's why it's funny."

We were in the lobby. I had the key, so I opened the door. The courtyard was quiet. My mother and I silently crossed it, then climbed the steps up to number 17. I opened the door and we hurried into the apartment.

Knowing the landlord had killed one person and tried to kill another gave the whole building an eerie feeling. I wanted to do what we needed to do and get out of there. I went directly to the desk, while my mother took the file out of her purse. I opened the lower drawer on the left, planning to tape the pages to the bottom of the drawer above. My mother handed them to me and I asked for the tape. That required another few moments rifling through her purse. I set the packet of papers on top of the files and waited.

"Here it is," she said, taking it out of her purse.

The door next to her cracked open.

"Hello?" Eddie said, as he gently pushed the door open. As subtly as I could I rested my hand on top of the xeroxed packet. "I saw you in the courtyard and thought I should come down and ask after Joanne."

"Oh, she's doing much better," my mother said. "She should be out—um, soon." I could see her deciding not to give the killer too much information.

"Well, good, I'm glad to hear that," he said. He didn't sound too sincere though. For a moment, it looked like he might leave. Then he opened the door wider and stepped in. "The police were here asking all sorts of questions about Allan and Tabitha."

"Were they?"

"I guess it's pretty certain they killed Rod. He disappeared and now she's gone too. That says something."

"I suppose it does."

"Jealousy is a terrible thing."

"It is."

"So, what are you doing here?" he asked. "I was under the impression you'd already taken all of Joanne's things to her."

I drew a blank. I couldn't think of a decent lie to tell him.

"Will," my mother said, choking a little. "Joanne asked us to look for Rod's will. She's going to need it."

"It's probably somewhere in the desk," he said, glancing down at my hand. I wasn't sure if he could figure out what I was trying to cover.

"Yes, I'm looking through the drawers."

He looked at us both, then gave an odd smile. "You know, it's strange that we were here at the party when Rod died. You know, Consuelo went to check on the kids and on the way back she noticed someone in Rod's window. She didn't think anything about it at the time. She thought—well, you know what she thought.

"You told me you weren't at the party," I said.

"No, I didn't say that."

"You said you were in San Diego Wednesday night."

"We left right after the party. Consuelo gets nervous before a trip and can't sleep, and if she can't sleep there's no point in my trying. We left around two-thirty. I mean, I guess that's technically Thursday morning, but it felt like Wednesday night. We got to San Diego around four fifteen."

That was interesting. So, he hadn't lied to me. And he and his wife must have told the police the truth about being there. That made me ask, "So, do you know how Rod found this place? Did you advertise in the *Weekly*?"

"Oh, um, no. I don't know how much you know about Rod's health, but he wasn't well. My wife and I actually invested—"

The sliding glass door slid open behind us. We turned to look at Consuelo standing there holding a gun in her hand. Joanne's gun; I could see the pearl grip.

"Honey, what are you doing?" Eddie asked.

"Why are you telling them everything?"

"Telling them—we have nothing to hide. Everything was done legal—" And then it seemed to hit him what it meant that his wife was standing there with a gun in her hand. "Consuelo, what did you do?"

"They're going to ruin everything. I have a friend on the way to take care of this."

"A friend?" her husband asked.

"One of my clients. He's going to take them out to the desert and—"

"Oh no!" Eddie yelled at her. "You're *not* going to do that!"

"It's the only way, Eddie. We can't let them ruin things. We have to get that money. We have to make a decent life for our kids."

"Not like that. Not by killing! Oh, Consuelo, what have you done?"

"I've done what you couldn't. I have taken care of my family."

"You killed Rod because he didn't die," I said, pushing the drawer closed and standing.

"He promised us. He promised us he'd die. The letter he got from his doctor said he wouldn't live until the end of 1991. It's almost the end of 1992 and he didn't even look sick. We couldn't keep waiting, we have three children to take care of."

"Why did you drug Joanne? She didn't suspect you."

"She thought she was the beneficiary. She wouldn't have gotten the money, but she would have held things up. Caused a problem. I couldn't let that happen."

"You're not a very patient person."

"Patient people end up with nothing."

Taking a step, I was standing in front of my mother. "Open the door," I said to her.

"Oh, no, you're not leaving here," Consuelo said. "Not alive."

"It's different, shooting someone who's looking at you. It's not like putting a pillow over someone's face. Or dropping drugged candy on a doorstep."

It was a guess on my part. I thought if she had the courage to shoot me face-to-face she'd have done it already. As it turns out, I was wrong. She aimed and pulled the trigger.

Eddie jumped in front of me and a moment later slumped against my chest, nearly knocking me over, and slid to the floor. Consuelo was screaming. She ran to Eddie, dropping the gun as she fell to the floor. My mother ran over and kicked the gun away like it was a disgusting rodent. Eddie was bleeding everywhere. I got on the floor with them and put my hands on his wound and pressed.

The front door opened and Javier ran in holding his gun in front of him.

"She was trying to shoot me, but her husband stepped in the way," I said, quickly. "She shot him instead."

Consuelo was still screaming, calling out Eddie's name. Javier grabbed her by an arm and dragged her to her feet. He said to me, "There are cuffs on my hip. Take them and handcuff her."

"No, no," Consuelo said.

Javier shook her and said, "If you give me any trouble I won't think twice before shooting you."

I took the handcuffs off his hip with my bloody hands. They opened easily and I slipped them over Consuelo's wrists, Javier guided her arms. She was compliant. Weak even. As though firing the gun had stolen all her strength.

"Call 911," Javier said to my mother. She stepped over to the phone on the desk and dialed. "Hello, yes, we need an ambulance and, um, backup."

"Why?! Why couldn't he just die like he was supposed to? None of this would have happened if he had just died."

Javier pushed Consuelo onto the couch, then got on his knees next to Eddie.

"Is he alive?" I asked.

"Barely. Can you get some towels?"

I hurried into the bathroom, feeling like I'd slipped into another world. I was in a stranger's bathroom grabbing towels for a dying man. Putting those thoughts aside, I rushed back out to the living room. Javier was putting pressure on Eddie's wound, asking if Eddie could hear him. Eddie seemed not to be hearing much of anything. Not even the approaching sirens getting closer and closer.

17

"OH MY GOD! WHAT HAPPENED?" MARC SCREAMED WHEN we got to the top of the red stairs. "You're covered in blood! Is it yours? No, it can't be yours, you're walking around. Did you kill someone?"

My mother and I sat down at the iron table and began to tell Marc and Louis everything that had happened while they poured us glasses of wine. It was after midnight.

We'd stayed at Rod's until the EMTs had taken Eddie away. He was still alive and it appeared, at least in that moment, that his wife would not be charged with another murder. As they were leaving, I asked Javier, "What are you doing here? You were supposed to be with your boyfriend."

"I got worried."

"But we didn't think there was anything to worry about."

"I know. I just…no matter what I do I can't stop thinking about you."

Then Amberson showed up. He glared at us like we'd done something horrible to him, when in reality all we'd done was solve his case. My mother glared right back and said, "There are three children alone in an apartment across the way. Do you mind if I go sit with them until someone arrives to take care of them?"

Amberson grumbled. Then he took Javier out onto the deck

and yelled at him for a while. I discretely went over to the desk, slipped the packet we'd stolen between two files and shut the drawer. Eventually we were going to have to explain what we were doing there in the first place.

Of course, I had no idea what to say about that. We could say we'd come to get something for Joanne, but visiting hours were over and she was coming home in morning.

I decided it might be a good idea to make myself unavailable for the moment. I walked out of the apartment and down into the courtyard past a couple of uniformed officers. Number 5 must have been standing in his doorway, because he was next to me as I walked by the pool.

"What happened?" he asked.

"Consuelo shot Eddie."

"Why would she do that?"

"She was trying to shoot me."

"Oh." Apparently that was a lot easier to understand.

"She's the one who killed Rod."

"Was he having sex with Eddie? You know, Eddie has always ticked my gaydar."

I briefly explained viatical insurance for the tenth time that week. Number 5 looked bored.

"So it was about greed," he said, clearly disappointed.

"Yes, it was about greed."

"Well, I never would have suspected that."

He'd followed me up the stairs to Eddie's apartment. "Mom," I called out when I stepped inside.

"Shhhhh! I just got the little ones settled," she whispered.

"We have to get out of here."

"What do you mean, dear?"

"Amberson is going to want a statement."

"Of course he is. I can't wait to tell him all the things that awful woman did."

"And all about why we were there," I said, raising an eyebrow.

"Oh. I see. Well, we can't leave these children alone."

I knew that made sense, although their parents seemed to

have no trouble leaving them alone. Of course, I suppose if you're committing crimes lack of childcare is not a stumbling block.

I looked at Number 5 and said, "You wouldn't mind…"

He blanched, but my mother jumped in and said, "Oh thank you! You're a lifesaver."

She picked up her purse and we scurried out of the apartment, leaving Number 5 stuck with the Castellon children.

On the way back to Silver Lake, we settled on a good story. It was simple and easy to remember. Joanne was supposed to be released, so we decided to go to the apartment and straighten up. Eddie stopped by to see how Joanne was, and we were chatting when his wife came in and threatened us with a gun.

"Why did she threaten us?" my mother asked.

"She thought we'd figured out that she'd killed Rod."

"Oh, that's good. It's almost true."

"I think the smart thing to do is to get you on your flight tomorrow, and then you can do a written statement in Grand Rapids and fax it to them. Do you think you can do that?"

"Don't worry. I'll contact a friend of mine who's a lawyer. He'll take care of it."

"You have a friend who's a lawyer?"

"Yes, I do."

That was odd. I didn't know she had friends I didn't know about. "What kind of friend?"

"You have your secrets and I have mine."

"Mom, after this visit I don't think I have any secrets left."

"Well, then I suggest you get busy."

After we'd told Marc and Louis everything, Louis said, "We should all go to bed, it's getting really late."

None of us moved though. Marc lit another cigarette and asked, "So, why didn't Rod die when he was supposed to?"

"I don't think they know enough about AIDS to tell you why one person dies quickly and another lives for years," Louis said.

"Hope," my mother said. "I think hope was keeping him alive."

"Well," Louis said, raising his glass. "Here's to hope."

EARLY THE NEXT MORNING, we put my mother's luggage into my tiny trunk and drove over to the hospital in Hollywood. The plan was we'd take Joanne back to Rod's apartment and then say our goodbyes. I assumed I'd have to offer her a hand over the next week or so. My mother would be very unhappy with me if I just abandoned the poor woman.

At the hospital, we were told Joanne was already in the lounge. As we walked down the hall toward the lounge, I saw that Joanne was sitting with a sour-looking woman of around forty. She had wide cheeks and wore her thin hair in bangs making her look like a very old ten-year-old. I assumed she was one of the psychologists, but after we said hello, Joanne said, "This is my daughter, Cindy."

"Oh hello," my mother said. "Joanne said you weren't able to come out. I'm so glad you could."

"She told me not to, but when I found out she was in this place I just had to come. What on earth has been going on?"

We tried explaining everything as briefly as possible. Some of it Joanne didn't know. Other things, like Rod's being HIV positive, I tried to leave out, but Joanne herself added that detail, so I launched ahead with my now well-rehearsed explanation of viatical settlements.

When I was finished, Cindy continued to look at us with suspicion. I had the feeling she was trying to find a way to blame us for the things that had happened to her mother, but we weren't responsible. Well, except for accidentally giving her sleeping pills instead of Valium.

"So, if my mother hadn't met you, she'd have had to go through this all alone?"

"I suppose. I mean, some of Rod's neighbors are actually nice. They might have helped."

"But she might be dead like my brother?"

"Well, it's hard to say what—"

"I'd be dead if the two of you hadn't come over when you did. That's what the doctor said." I hadn't heard that and wasn't quite sure Joanne wasn't saying it so her daughter would like us. If that was the case, it worked. Cindy stood up—she was quite tall actually—and pulled both my mother and myself into a big sweaty hug. When we finally pulled apart, I decided I should move things along.

"Are they discharging Joanne soon? We can give you a ride to the apartment."

"I rented a car at the airport," Cindy said.

"And they're taking forever letting me out of here," Joanne said, grumpily.

"Well, we should probably head out to the airport then." To Cindy I said, "Your mother has my phone number if there's anything I can do. I used to live over this way, so I know where everything is, all the good restaurants and stuff."

"Thank you. I'm sure we'll muddle through." I was fairly certain Cindy would not be calling me. I don't think she disliked me exactly, but I did think that her mother had probably picked up a lot of strange people over the years. Cindy would avoid me, not out of malice but out of habit.

My mother gave Joanne a big hug and said, "I'm so glad I met you. You call me when you get back home. You know, we're really not that far apart. We could meet in the middle and have lunch."

"Is that Kalamazoo?"

"Yes, it is."

"Well, we should; we should do that."

After that there was little to say, so we bid our final good-byes and left. Traffic was light since it was midday and people were taking an extra day off after the holiday. We were cruising at about forty miles an hour on the 10 West, when my mother said, "Well, it certainly was an interesting visit."

"It was, wasn't it."

"It was exhilarating, investigating a murder. I can see why you do it. It must make you feel very alive."

"Actually, I try hard not to do it, Mom. It's just, well, my friends get interested and I just sort of get carried away."

"You know, you probably don't remember this, but they used to show Perry Mason every afternoon when you got home from school. I liked it, but I hated watching it with you. I finally gave up."

"Why did you hate watching it with me?"

"Because you always knew who the killer was twenty minutes in. Maybe you were meant to do these things."

"Mom, I'd probably figured out the show's formula. Just because I could figure out the killer on Perry Mason doesn't mean I'm a natural detective."

"Doesn't it? I don't know."

We passed the La Brea exit, which made me think of the tar pits, which I'd never seen, and I said to my mother, "You'll have to come back soon and we'll do more actual sightseeing."

"That sounds lovely. And you need to come home. For a visit. Just a visit." Her voice was a tad winsome. I was afraid she was about to start crying. There was nothing worse than crying on the freeway in L.A., especially if you're just visiting.

When we got to LAX, I was heading to Terminal Four to park when my mother said, "No, please don't park. I'm just going to jump out and that's that."

"Mom, I can wait with you."

"No, I don't think I want you to."

I changed lanes a little too quickly for the car behind us, getting us honked at, and then I pulled up in front of the American Airlines gate. I got out and went around to the back to open the trunk. My mother waved at a skycap to grab her bags for her.

"I really feel like I should wait with you. Your flight is almost two hours from now."

"Oh that's all right, I think I might wait in one of the bars. Who knows what might happen?" She winked at me, squeezed me tight and then ran off.

I SAT on the examining table feeling bloated. I'd had a lot of time to kill between dropping my mother off and my appointment, but it wasn't so much time that it was worth going all the way home and then coming out again later. I'd stopped at Pann's and had an early lunch. I'd eaten an entire patty melt, all of my fries and gotten refills on my Coke. Sitting there, I was regretting my sudden dive into gluttony.

Dr. Sam came into the room. He was an attractive, blue-eyed blond. He was almost attractive enough to play a doctor on television. His nose was buried in my file, which was much thicker than I would have liked.

"Your tests look very good. I'm very happy. There's a small decline in your T-cell count. I'm not at all worried about it."

I was tempted to say, "Yeah, but they're not your T-cells" but I didn't. Instead, I uttered that very useful standby, "Uh-huh."

"Your red blood cells look good. Are you feeling less run down?"

"Yeah, I think so."

"Good. Why don't I look around a little bit?" Then he felt around my neck and my collarbones and under my jaw. He lifted my arms and he felt around under there. He did the same with my upper thighs. Then he told me to lie down and he felt around my stomach. I'm ticklish, so I giggled a few times.

"Sorry," I said, catching my breath.

"No, that's fine. I'd much rather hear you giggle than screaming in pain."

That immediately sobered me. I didn't like knowing screaming in pain was on the possibility list.

"So, I've talked to some people who think AZT isn't helping."

He stopped what he was doing and sighed. "It seems to help. And it's pretty much all we have right now. I mean, we have DDC and DDI, but both are less effective."

"Then why do you ever give anyone DDC and DD—"

"I, DDI. We give those to people who absolutely can't tolerate AZT. Are you having trouble with AZT?"

"I feel like I've been forgetting things," I said without thinking.

"And you think that's related to AZT?"

"Um, I don't know. What do you think?"

"It's not listed as a side effect. Though you're hardly the first patient I've had mention forgetfulness. Are you depressed?"

"No. I'm not. I mean, I don't think so."

Suddenly, I wondered, was I really forgetting things? I'd forgotten Joanne's last name a few times, and Eddie's, and the name of the investment company—though I'd only glanced at that once, so I shouldn't really expect to remember it.

"Actually, I think I'm doing better. Maybe the forgetting isn't a big deal."

He looked over the file and gave me a smile. "You know, a lot of my patients become hyper-aware of their health. It's pretty natural."

I was fairly certain he'd just called me a hypochondriac without using the word.

"Are you still keeping things to yourself?"

"I've told more people about what's going on with me. Well, I've told my mother."

"And the two of you talk about it?"

"Oh yeah," I said, quickly. Too quickly. We talked about it, but mostly about what she felt. Which was fine; I didn't want to talk about what I felt. I was afraid it would just make it harder for her.

"Okay, well, keep an eye on the forgetfulness and let me know next time if it's getting worse. We can do some tests if it is. In the meantime, you need to talk about how you feel."

"With you?"

"I wish I could say yes, but I have four patients waiting."

"Oh, okay. I'll figure it out."

On the way out of Dr. Sam's office, I stopped at the window and wrote a check for my co-pay. I almost walked away without my checkbook, which didn't help my fears about being more forgetful. I did remember to have my parking validated, so maybe I was exaggerating my fear. Maybe I wasn't forgetting things any more than anyone else. Maybe there was nothing wrong with my memory. Dr. Sam might be right. I was paying too much attention to my health.

After I retrieved my car, I took Wilshire over to Doheny and then went north to Santa Monica. There were no freeways nearby, so the best way to get home was using surface streets. That took me through the heart of West Hollywood past Rage and Revolver and all the other bars. There was a gym where the membership was almost a hundred percent gay, and as I drove by I could see the muscle queens in bike shorts and cut-off tank tops coming and going.

I was almost out of West Hollywood, when I pulled over and parked. I hadn't really been planning to, but I thought, "Why not?"

Climbing out of the car, I crossed the street to the West Hollywood Universal Church. Walking through the front door, I saw that the nave had been reorganized so the chairs were in a circle. Most of them were occupied. C.B. was sitting in one of them on the far side, so he saw me the minute I walked in. His smiled broadened. Still, I lingered at the door because one of the guys was talking.

"—we're talking, you know, and connecting, really connecting, and I'm thinking I've gotta tell him, I've gotta tell him soon. But I know it's going to ruin everything and it feels so good to just talk to a nice guy, a guy who really seems to hear me, you know? And then, like, before I can tell him he says, 'I'm so glad to meet someone who's obviously okay,' because the last two guys he tried to date had AIDS. And then I just got up and walked away, because there was nothing to say after that."

The others in the group offered a few encouraging words. Mostly that the guy he liked was an asshole and it was good to find out right up front.

Then C.B. said, "Guys, we have someone new joining us." He waved me into the room and said to me, "Have a seat. And tell everyone who you are."

I went to an empty chair and sat down.

"Um, my name is Noah."

LOUIS' THANKSGIVING DAY MENU

Appetizers
Fried Ravioli with Aioli Dip
Mini Blue Corn Pancakes served with
Caviar, Sour Cream and Lemon Zest
Relish Tray

Soup
Carrot, Apple, Ginger

Salad
Field Greens with Blue Cheese, Bacon and Cherry Tomatoes
Raspberry Vinaigrette Dressing

Entrée
Brined Turkey
Gravy & Sausage Dressing
Mashed Potatoes
Sweet Potato Casserole
Green Bean Casserole
Creamed Peas, Mushrooms and Onions
Cranberry Sauce
Biscuits

Louis' Thanksgiving Day Menu

Dessert
Three-Layer Pumpkin Pie (chilled)

LOUIS' THREE-LAYER PUMPKIN PIE

Make your favorite pie crust. It can be regular, whole wheat or a crumb crust with ginger snaps. Whatever you like. Next time I make this I'm going to try chocolate cookies.

Make your favorite pumpkin pie recipe. I use the one on the can. I leave out the cloves because I always forget to buy them. I add a little nutmeg instead.

Pour half of the filling into the pie crust. Pour the other half in to a glass dish that you've greased or sprayed with Pam.

The recipe will probably tell you to start out at 425 degrees and then turn it down to 350 after fifteen minutes. Don't do that. The reason to do that is so that you get a nice skin on the pie, you don't need that for this pie. And since the filling is much thinner, it will only take about a half an hour in the oven. Stick a knife in when you think it's done. If it comes out clean it's done.

Allow the pie and the filling to cool. When it's cool, beat a cup of it to a cup and a half of whipping cream until stiff. The amount of cream depends on the size of your pie pan. If you're using a deep dish, go with the larger amount. Scrape the filling from the sides of the glass dish and then slowly add it to the whipped cream. Continue to beat. When you've added all the filling, you should have a nice, stiff, light orange layer. Spread that over the pie.

Now, beat a cup and a half of whipping cream until stiff. You can add a teaspoon of sugar, vanilla to taste, and perhaps a little bit of cinnamon before you start. If you want to go restaurant-style and make whipped cream that will last through the apocalypse, add gelatin at this stage. No need to add gelatin to the middle layer, since it will already stay nice and stiff. Spread the whipped cream onto the pie.

Sprinkle toasted walnuts on top. Or chocolate shavings if you've gone with a chocolate crust. Or crumbled ginger snaps— or be creative!

You can also adapt this process to Coconut Cream pie, Chocolate Cream pie, or Banana Cream pie.

ALSO BY MARSHALL THORNTON

My Favorite Uncle

Femme

Praline Goes to Washington

Aunt Belle's Time Travel & Collectibles

Masc

Never Rest

ABOUT THE AUTHOR

Marshall Thornton writes two popular mystery series, the *Boys-town Mysteries* and the *Pinx Video Mysteries*. He has won the Lambda Award for Gay Mystery twice, once for each series. His romantic comedy, *Femme* was also a 2016 Lambda finalist for Best Gay Romance. Other books include *My Favorite Uncle*, *The Ghost Slept Over* and *Masc,* the sequel to *Femme.* He is a member of Mystery Writers of America.

CPSIA information can be obtained
at www.ICGtesting.com
Printed in the USA
LVHW042257270619
622622LV00001B/5/P